THE
PAST IS RED

....

ALSO BY CATHERYNNE M. VALENTE

The Labyrinth
Yume No Hon: The Book of Dreams
The Grass-Cutting Sword
Under In The Mere
Palimpsest
Silently and Very Fast
Deathless
Six-Gun Snow White
Radiance
The Refrigerator Monologues
The Glass Town Game
Space Opera
Mass Effect: Annihilation
Minecraft: The End

FAIRYLAND

The Girl Who Circumnavigated Fairyland in a Ship of Her Own Making
The Girl Who Fell Beneath Fairyland and Led the Revels There
The Girl Who Soared Over Fairyland and Cut the Moon in Two
The Boy Who Lost Fairyland
The Girl Who Raced Fairyland All the Way Home

THE ORPHAN'S TALES

The Orphan's Tales: In the Night Garden
The Orphan's Tales: In the Cities of Coin and Spice

A DIRGE FOR PRESTER JOHN

The Habitation of the Blessed
The Folded World

SHORT FICTION COLLECTIONS

The Bread We Eat in Dreams
Myths of Origin
The Melancholy of Mechagirl
The Future Is Blue

THE
PAST IS RED

· ·

CATHERYNNE M. VALENTE

TOR
DOT
COM

A TOM DOHERTY ASSOCIATES BOOK

NEW YORK

THE PAST IS RED

Edited by Jonathan Strahan

A Tordotcom Book
Published by Tom Doherty Associates
120 Broadway
New York, NY 10271

www.tor.com

Tor® is a registered trademark of Macmillan Publishing Group, LLC.

The Library of Congress Cataloging-in-Publication Data
is available upon request.

ISBN 978-1-250-30113-0 (hardcover)
ISBN 978-1-250-30112-3 (ebook)

Our books may be purchased in bulk for promotional, educational, or business use. Please contact your local bookseller or the Macmillan Corporate and Premium Sales Department at 1-800-221-7945, extension 5442, or by email at MacmillanSpecialMarkets@macmillan.com.

First Edition: July 2021

Printed in the United States of America

0 9 8 7 6 5 4 3 2 1

For caroll spinney

part I

THE FUTURE IS BLUE

NIHILIST

. . . .

MY NAME IS Tetley Abednego and I am the most hated girl in Garbagetown. I am nineteen years old. I live alone in Candle Hole, where I was born, and have no friends except for a deformed gannet bird I've named Grape Crush and a motherless elephant seal cub I've named Big Bargains, and also the hibiscus flower that has recently decided to grow out of my roof, but I haven't named it anything yet. I love encyclopedias, a cassette I found when I was eight that says *Madeline Brix's Superboss Mixtape '97* on it in very nice handwriting, plays by Mr. Shakespeare or Mr. Webster or Mr. Beckett, lipstick, Garbagetown, and my twin brother, Maruchan. Maruchan is the only thing that loves me back, but he's my twin, so it doesn't really count. We couldn't stop loving each other any more than the sea could stop being so greedy and give us back China or drive time radio or polar bears.

But he doesn't visit anymore.

When we were little, Maruchan and I always asked each other the same question before bed. Every night, we crawled into the Us-Fort together—an impregnable stronghold of a bed we had nailed up ourselves out of the carcasses of several hacked-apart bassinets, prams, and cradles. It took up the whole of our bedroom. No one could see us in there, once we closed the porthole (a manhole cover I swiped from Scrapmetal Abbey stamped with stars, a crescent moon, and the magic words NEW ORLEANS WATER METER), and we felt certain no one could hear us, either. We lay together under our canopy of moldy green lace and shredded buggy-hoods and mobiles with only one shattered fairy fish remaining. Sometimes I asked first and sometimes he did, but we never gave the same answer twice.

"Maruchan, what do you want to be when you grow up?"

He would give it a serious think. Once, I remember, he whispered:

"When I grow up I want to be the Thames!"

"Whatever for?" I giggled.

"Because the Thames got so big and so bossy and so strong that it ate London all up in one go! Nobody tells a Thames what to do or who to eat. A Thames tells *you*. Imagine having a whole city to eat, and not having to share any! Also there were millions of eels in the Thames and I only get to eat eels at Easter, which isn't fair when I want to eat them all the time."

And he pretended to bite me and eat me all up.

"Very well, you shall be the Thames and I shall be the Mississippi and together we shall eat up the whole world."

Then we'd go to sleep and dream the same dreams. We always dreamed the same dreams, which was like living twice.

After that, whenever we were hungry, which was always all the time and forever, we'd say *We're bound for London-town!* until we drove our parents so mad that they forbade the word *London* in the house, but you can't forbid a word, so there.

EVERY MORNING I wake up to find words painted on my door like toadstools popping up in the night.

Today it says NIHILIST in big black letters. That's not so bad! It's almost sweet! Big Bargains flumps toward me on her fat seal-belly while I light the wicks on my beeswax door, and we watch them burn together until the word melts away.

"I don't think I'm a nihilist, Big Bargains. Do you?"

She rolls over onto my matchbox stash so that I'll rub her stomach. Rubbing a seal's stomach is the opposite of nihilism.

Yesterday, an old man hobbled up over a ridge of rusted bicycles and punched me so hard he broke my nose. By law, I had to let him. I had to say: *Thank you, Grandfather, for my instruction.* I had to stand there and wait in case he wanted to do something else to me. Anything but kill me; those were his rights. But he didn't want more, he just wanted to cry and ask me why I did it and the law doesn't say I have to answer that, so I just stared at him until he went away. Once a gang of schoolgirls shaved off all my hair and wrote CUNT in blue marker on the back of my skull. *Thank you, sisters, for my instruction.* The schoolboys do worse. After graduation they come round and eat my food and hold me down and try to make me cry, which I never do. It's their rite of passage. *Thank you, brothers, for my instruction.*

But other than that, I'm really a very happy person! I'm awfully lucky when you think about it. Garbagetown is the most wonderful place anybody has ever lived in the history of the world, even if you count the Pyramids and New York City and Camelot. I have Grape Crush and Big Bargains and my hibiscus flower, and I can fish like I've got bait for a heart so I hardly ever go hungry, and once I found a ruby ring *and* a New Mexico license plate inside a bluefin tuna. Everyone says they only hate me because I annihilated hope and butchered our future, but I know better, and anyway, it's a lie. Some people are just born to be despised. The Loathing of Tetley began small and grew bigger and bigger, like the Thames, until it swallowed me whole.

Maruchan and I were born fifty years after the Great Sorting, which is another lucky thing that happened to me. After all, I could have been born a Fuckwit and gotten drowned with all the rest of them, or I could have grown up on a Misery Boat, sailing around hopelessly looking for land, or one of the first to realize people could live on a patch of garbage in the Pacific Ocean the size of the place that used to be called Texas, or I could have been a Sorter and spent my whole life moving rubbish from one end of the patch to the other so that a pile of crap could turn into a country and babies could be born in places like Candle Hole or Scrapmetal Abbey or Pill Hill or Toyside or Teagate.

Candle Hole is the most beautiful place in Garbagetown, which is the most beautiful place in the world. All the stubs of candles the Fuckwits threw out piled up into hills and mountains and caverns and dells, votive candles and taper candles and tea lights and birthday candles and big fat colorful pillar candles, stacked and somewhat melted into a great crumbling gorgeous warren of wicks and wax. All the houses are cozy little honeycombs melted into the hillside, with smooth round windows and low golden ceilings. At night, from far away, Candle Hole looks like a firefly palace. When the wind blows, it smells like cinnamon, and freesia, and cranberries, and lavender, and Fresh Linen Scent, and New Car Smell.

тне тerriвLe power oF FUCKWIT CaKe

. . . .

OUR PARENTS' NAMES are Life and Time. Time lay down on her Fresh Linen Scent wax bed and I came out of her first, then Maruchan. But even though I got here first, I came out blue as the ocean, not breathing, with the umbilical cord wrapped round my neck and Maruchan wailing, still squeezing my noose with his tiny fist, like he was trying to get me free. Doctor Pimms unstrangled and unblued me and put me in a Hawaiian Fantasies–scented wax hollow in our living room. I lay there alone, too startled by living to cry, until the sun came up and Life and Time remembered I had survived. Maruchan was so healthy and sweet natured and strong and, even though Garbagetown is the most beautiful place in the world, many children don't live past a year or two. We don't even get names until we turn ten. (Before that, we answer happily to Girl or Boy or Child or Darling.) Better to focus on the one that will grow up rather than get attached to the sickly poor beast who hasn't got a chance.

I was born already a ghost. But I was a very noisy ghost. I screamed and wept at all hours while Life and Time waited for me to die. I only nursed when my brother was full, I only played with toys he forgot, I only spoke after he had spoken. Maruchan said his first word at the supper table: *please*. What a lovely, polite word for a lovely, polite child! After they finished cooing over him, I very calmly turned to my mother and said: *Mama, may I have a scoop of mackerel roe? It is my favorite.* I thought they would be so proud! After all, I made twelve more words than my brother. This was my moment, the wonderful moment when they would realize that they did love me and I wasn't going to die and I was special and good. But everyone got very quiet. They were not happy that the ghost could talk. I had been able to for ages, but everything in my world said to wait for my brother before I could do anything at all. *No, you may not have mackerel roe, because you are a deceitful wicked little show-off child.*

When we turned ten, we went to fetch our names. This is just the most terribly exciting thing for a Garbagetown kid. At ten, you are a real person. At ten, people want to know you. At ten, you will probably live for a good while yet. This is how you catch a name: wake up to the fabulous new world of being ten and greet your birthday Frankencake (a hodgepodge of well-preserved Fuckwit snack cakes filled with various cremes and jellies). Choose a slice, with much fanfare. Inside, your adoring and/or neglectful mother will have hidden various small objects—an aluminum pull tab, a medicine bottle cap, a broken earring, a coffee bean, a wee striped capacitor, a tiny plastic rocking horse, maybe a postage stamp. Remove said item from your mouth without cutting yourself or eating it. Now, walk in the direction of your prize. Toward Aluminumopolis or Pill Hill or Spanglestoke or Teagate or Electric City or Toyside or Lost Post Gulch. Walk and walk and walk. Never once brush yourself off or wash in the ocean, even after camping on a pile of magazines or wishbones or pregnancy tests or wrapping paper with glitter reindeer on it. Walk until nobody knows you. When, finally, a stranger hollers at you to get out of the way or go back where you came from or stop stealing the good rubbish, they will, without even realizing, call you by your true name, and you can begin to pick and stumble your way home.

My brother grabbed a chocolate snack cake with a curlicue of white icing on it. I chose a pink and red tigery striped hunk of cake filled with gooshy creme de something. The sugar hit our brains like twin tsunamis. He spat out a little gold earring with the post broken off. I felt a smooth, hard gelcap lozenge in my mouth. Pill Hill it was then, and the great mountain of Fuckwit anxiety medication. But when I carefully pulled the thing out, it was a little beige capacitor with red stripes instead. Electric City! I'd never been half so far. Richies lived in Electric City. Richies and brightboys and dazzlegirls and kerosene kings. My brother was off in the opposite direction, toward Spanglestoke and the desert of engagement rings.

Maybe none of it would have happened if I'd gone to Spanglestoke for my name instead. If I'd never seen the gasoline gardens of Engine Row. If I'd gone home straightaway after finding my name. If I'd never met Goodnight Moon in the brambles of Hazmat Heath with all the garbage stars rotting gorgeously overhead. Such is the terrible power of Fuckwit Cake.

I walked cheerfully out of Candle Hole with my St. Oscar backpack strapped on tight and didn't look back once. Why should I? St. Oscar had my back. I'm not really that religious nowadays. But everyone's religious when they're ten. St. Oscar was a fuzzy green Fuckwit man who lived in a garbage can just like me, and frowned a lot just like me. He understood me and loved me and knew how to bring civilization out of trash, and I loved him back even though he was a Fuckwit. Nobody chooses how they get born. Not even Oscar.

So I scrambled up over the wax ridges of my home and into the world with Oscar on my back. The Matchbox Forest rose up around me: towers of EZ Strike matchbooks and boxes from impossible, magical places like the Coronado

Hotel, Becky's Diner, the Fox and Hound Pub. Garbage-towners picked through heaps and cairns of blackened, used matchsticks looking for the precious ones that still had their red and blue heads intact. But I knew all those pickers. They couldn't give me a name. I waved at the hot-heads. I climbed up Flintwheel Hill, my feet slipping and sliding on the mountain of spent butane lighters, until I could see out over all of Garbagetown just as the broiling cough drop–red sun was setting over Far Boozeaway, hit-ting the crystal bluffs of stockpiled whiskey and gin bot-tles and exploding into a billion billion rubies tumbling down into the hungry sea.

I sang a song from school to the sun and the matchsticks. It's an ask-and-answer song, so I had to sing both parts my-self, which feels very odd when you have always had a twin to do the asking or the answering, but I didn't mind.

> Who liked it hot and hated snow?
> The Fuckwits did! The Fuckwits did!
> Who ate up every thing that grows?
> The Fuckwits did! The Fuckwits did!
> Who drowned the world in oceans blue?
> The Fuckwits did! The Fuckwits did!
> Who took the land from me and you?
> The Fuckwits did, we know it's true!
> Are YOU Fuckwits, children dear?
> We're GARBAGETOWNERS, free and clear!
> But who made the garbage, rich and rank?
> The Fuckwits did, and we give thanks.

The Lawn stretched out below me, full of the grass clip-pings and autumn leaves and fallen branches and banana peels and weeds and gnawed bones and eggshells of the fer-tile Fuckwit world, slowly turning into the gold of Garbagetown: soil. Real earth. Terra bloody firma. We can already grow rice in the dells. And here and there, big, blowsy flowers bang up out of the rot: hibiscus, African tulips, bitter gourds, a couple of purple lotuses floating in the damp mucky bits. I slept next to a blue and white orchid that looked like my brother's face.

"Orchid, what do you want to be when you grow up?" I whispered to it. In real life, it didn't say anything back. It just fluttered a little in the moonlight and the sea wind. But when I got around to dreaming, I dreamed about the orchid, and it said: *a farm*.

3

MURDERCUNT

· · · · · · · · · · · · · ·

IN GARBAGETOWN, YOU think real hard about what you're gonna eat next, where the fresh water's at, and where you're gonna sleep. Once all that's settled you can whack your mind on nicer stuff, like gannets and elephant seals and what to write next on the Bitch of Candle Hole's door. (This morning I melted MURDERCUNT off the back wall of my house. Big Bargains flopped down next to me and watched the blocky red painted letters swirl and fade into the Buttercream Birthday Cake wax. Maybe I'll name my hibiscus flower Murdercunt. It has a nice big sound.)

When I remember hunting my name, I mostly remember the places I slept. It's a real dog to find good spots. Someplace sheltered from the wind, without too much seawater seep, where no one'll yell at you for wastreling on their patch or try to stick it in you in the middle of the night just because you're all alone and it looks like you probably don't have a knife.

I always have a knife.

So I slept with St. Oscar the Grouch for my pillow, in the shadow of a mountain of black chess pieces in Gamegrange, under a thicket of tabloids and *Wall Street Journals* and remaindered novels with their covers torn off in Bookbury, snuggled into a spaghetti-pile of unspooled cassette ribbon on the outskirts of the Sound Downs, on the lee side of a little soggy Earl Grey hillock in Teagate. In the morning I sucked on a few of the teabags, and the dew on them tasted like the loveliest cuppa any Fuckwit ever poured his stupid self. I said my prayers on beds of old microwaves and moldy photographs of girls with perfect hair kissing at the camera. *St. Oscar, keep your mighty lid closed over me. Look grouchily but kindly upon me and protect me as I travel through the infinite trashcan of your world. Show me the beautiful usefulness of your Blessed Rubbish. Let me not be Taken Out before I find my destiny.*

But my destiny didn't seem to want to find me. As far as I walked, I still saw people I knew. Mr. Zhu raking his mushroom garden, nestled in a windbreak of broken milk bottles. Miss Amancharia gave me one of the coconut crabs out of her nets, which was very nice of her, but hardly a name. Even as far away as Teagate, I saw Tropicana Sita welding a refrigerator door to a hull-metal shack. She flipped up her mask and waved at me. Dammit! She was Allsorts Sita's cousin, and Allsorts drank with my mother every Thursday at the Black Wick.

By the time I walked out of Teagate I'd been gone eight days. I was getting pretty ripe. Bits and pieces of Garbagetown were stuck all over my clothes, but no tidying up. Them's the rules. I could see the blue crackle of Electric City sparkling up out of the richie-rich Coffee Bean Burbs. Teetering towers of batteries rose up like desert hoodoo spires—AA, AAA, 12-volt, DD, car, solar, lithium, anything you like. Parrots and pelicans screamed down the battery canyons, their talons kicking off sprays of AAAs that tumbled down the heights like rockslides. Sleepy banks of generators rumbled pleasantly along a river of wires and extension cords and HDMI cables. Fields of delicate lightbulbs windchimed in the breeze. Anything that had a working engine lived here. Anything that still had *juice*. If Garbagetown had a heart, it was Electric City. Electric City pumped power. Power and privilege.

In Electric City, the lights of the Fuckwit world were still on.

4

GOODNIGHT GARBAGETOWN

. . . .

"OI, TETLEY! FUCK off back home to your darkhole! We're full up on little cunts here!"

And that's how I got my name. Barely past the battery spires of Electric City, a fat gas-huffing fucksack voltage jockey called me a little cunt. But he also called me Tetley. He brayed it down from a pyramid of telephones, and his friends all laughed and drank homebrew out of a glass jug and went back to not working. I looked down—among the many scraps of rubbish clinging to my shirt and pants and backpack and hair was a bright blue teabag wrapper with TETLEY CLASSIC BLEND BLACK TEA written on it in cheerful white letters, clinging to my chest.

I tried to feel the power of my new name. The *me*-ness of it. I tried to imagine my mother and father when they were young, waking up with some torn-out page of *Life* or *Time* magazine stuck to their rears, not even noticing until someone barked out their whole lives for a laugh. But I couldn't feel anything while the volt-humpers kept on staring at me like I was nothing but a used-up potato battery. I didn't even know then that the worst swear word in Electric City was *dark*. I didn't know they were waiting to see how mad I'd get 'cause they called my home a darkhole. I didn't care. They were wrong and stupid. Except for the hole part. Candle Hole never met a dark it couldn't burn down.

Maybe I should have gone home right then. I had my name! Time to hoof it back over the river and through the woods, girl. But I'd never seen Electric City and it was morning and if I stayed gone a while longer maybe they'd miss me. Maybe they'd worry. And maybe now they'd love me, now that I was a person with a name. Maybe I could even filch a couple of batteries or a cup of gasoline and turn up at my parents' door in turbo-powered triumph. I'd tell my brother all my adventures and he'd look at me like I was magic on a stick and everything would be good forever and ever, amen.

So I wandered. I gawped. It was like being in school and learning the Fuckwit song, only I was walking around *inside* the Fuckwit song and it was all still happening right now everywhere. Electric City burbled and bubbled and clanged and belched and smoked just like the bad old world before it all turned blue. Everyone had such fine things! I saw a girl wearing a ballgown out of a fairy book, green and glitter and miles of ruffles, and she wasn't even *going* anywhere. She was just tending her gasoline garden out the back of her little cottage, which wasn't made out of candles or picturebooks or cat food cans, but real cottage parts! Mostly doors and shutters and really rather a lot of windows, but they fit together like they never even needed the other parts of a house in the first place. And the girl in her greenglitter dress carried a big red watering can around her garden, sprinkling fuel stabilizer into her tidy rows of petrol barrels and gas cans with their graceful spouts pointed toward the sun. Why not wear that dress all the time? Just a wineglass full of what she was growing in her garden would buy almost anything in Garbagetown. She smiled shyly at me. I hated her. And I wanted to be her.

By afternoon I was bound for London-town, so hungry I could've slurped up every eel the Thames ever had. There's no food lying around in Electric City. In Candle Hole I could've grabbed candy or a rice ball or jerky off any old midden heap. But here everybody owned their piece and kept it real neat, *mercilessly* neat, and they didn't share. I sat down on a rusty Toyota transmission and fished around in my backpack for crumbs. My engine sat on one side of a huge cyclone fence. I'd never seen one all put together before. Sure, you find torn-off shreds of wire fences, but this one was all grown up, with proper locks and chain wire all over it. It meant to Keep You Out. Inside, like hungry dogs, endless barrels and freezers and cylinders and vats went on and on, with angry writing on them that said HAZMAT or BIOHAZARD or RADIOACTIVE or WARNING or DANGER or CLASSIFIED.

"Got anything good in there?" said a boy's voice. I looked round and saw a kid my own age, with wavy black hair and big brown eyes and three little moles on his forehead. He was wearing the nicest clothes I ever saw on a boy—a blue suit that almost, *almost* fit him. With a *tie*.

"Naw," I answered. "Just a dry sweater, an empty can of Cheez Whiz, some souvenirs from home, and *Madeline Brix's Superboss Mixtape '97.* It's my good luck charm." I showed him my beloved mixtape. Madeline Brix made all the dots on her *i*'s into hearts. It was a totally Fuckwit thing to do and I loved her for it even though she was dead and didn't care if I loved her or not.

"*Cool,*" the boy said, and I could tell he meant it. He didn't even call me a little cunt or anything. He pushed his thick hair out of his face. "Listen, you really shouldn't be here. No one's gonna say anything because you're not Electrified, but it's so completely dangerous. They put all that stuff in one place so it couldn't get out and hurt anyone."

"Electrified?"

"One of us. Local." He had the decency to look embarrassed. "Anyway, I saw you and I thought that if some crazy darkgirl is gonna have a picnic on Hazmat Heath, I could at least help her not die while she's doing it."

The boy held out his hand. He was holding a gas mask. He showed me how to fasten it under my hair. The sun started to set rosily behind a tangled briar of motherboards. Everything turned pink and gold and slow and sleepy. I climbed down from my engine tuffet and lay under the fence next to the boy in the suit. He'd brought a mask for himself, too. We looked at each other through the eye holes.

"My name's Goodnight Moon," he said.

"Mine's . . ." And I did feel my new name swirling up inside me then, like good tea, like cream and sugar cubes, like the most essential me. "Tetley."

"I'm sorry I called you a darkgirl, Tetley."

"Why?"

"It's not a nice thing to call someone."

"I like it. It sounds pretty."

"It isn't. I promise. Do you forgive me?"

I tugged on the hose of my gas mask. The air coming through tasted like nickels. "Sure. I'm aces at forgiving. Been practicing all my life. Besides . . ." My turn to go red in the face. "At the Black Wick they'd probably call you a brightboy and that's not as pretty as it sounds, either."

Goodnight Moon's brown eyes stared out at me from behind thick glass. It was the closest I'd ever been to a boy who wasn't my twin. Goodnight Moon didn't feel like a twin. He felt like the opposite of a twin. We never shared a womb, but on the other end of it all, we might still share a grave. His tie was burgundy with green swirls in it. He hadn't tied it very well, so I could see the skin of his throat, which was very clean and probably very soft.

"Hey," he said, "do you want to hear your tape?"

"What do you mean, *hear* it? It's not for hearing, it's for luck."

Goodnight Moon laughed. His laugh burst all over me like butterfly bombs. He reached into his suit jacket and pulled out a thick black rectangle. I handed him *Madeline Brix's Superboss Mixtape '97* and he hit a button on the side of the rectangle. It popped open; Goodnight Moon slotted in my tape and handed me one end of a long wire.

"Put it in your ear," he said, and I did.

A man's voice filled up my head from my jawbone up to the plates of my skull. The most beautiful and saddest voice that ever was. A voice like Candle Hole all lit up at twilight. A voice like the whole old world calling up from the bottom of the sea. The man on Madeline Brix's tape was saying he was happy, and he hoped I was happy, too.

Goodnight Moon reached out to hold my hand just as the sky went black and starry. I was crying. He was, too. Our tears dripped out of our gas masks onto the rusty road of Electric City.

When the tape ended, I dug in my backpack for a match and a stump of candle: dark red, Holiday Memories scent. I lit it at the same moment that Goodnight Moon pulled a little flashlight out of his pocket and turned it on. We held our glowings between us. We were the same.

BRIGHTBITCH

. . . .

ALLSORTS SITA CAME to visit me today. Clicked my knocker early in the morning, early enough that I could be sure she'd never slept in the first place. I opened for her, as I am required to do. She looked up at me with eyes like bullet holes, leaning on my waxy hinges, against the T in BRIGHT-BITCH, thoughtfully scrawled in what appeared to be human shit across the front of my hut. BRIGHTBITCH smelled, but Allsorts Sita smelled worse. Her breath punched me in the nose before she did. I got a lungful of what Diet Sprite down at the Black Wick optimistically called "cognac": the thick pinkish booze you could get by extracting the fragrance oil and preservatives out of candles and mixing it with wood alcohol the kids over in Furnitureford boiled out of dining sets and china cabinets. Smells like flowers vomited all over a New Car and then killed a badger in the backseat. Allsorts Sita looked like she'd drunk so much cognac you could light one strand of her hair and she'd burn for eight days.

"You fucking whore," she slurred.

"Thank you, Auntie, for my instruction," I answered quietly.

I have a place I go to in my mind when I have visitors who aren't seals or gannet birds or hibiscus flowers. A little house made all of doors and windows, where I wear a greenglitter dress every day and water my gas-can garden and read by electric light.

"I hate you. I hate you. How could you do it? We raised

you and fed you and this is how you repay it all. You ungrateful bitch."

"Thank you, Auntie, for my instruction."

In my head I ran my fingers along a cyclone fence and all the barrels on the other side read LIFE and LOVE and FORGIVENESS and UNDERSTANDING.

"You've killed us all," Allsorts Sita moaned. She puked up magenta cognac on my stoop. When she was done puking she hit me over and over with closed fists. It didn't hurt too much. Allsorts is a small woman. But it hurt when she clawed my face and my breasts with her fingernails. Blood came up like wax spilling, and when she finished she passed out cold, halfway in my house, halfway out.

"Thank you, Auntie, for my instruction," I said to her sleeping body. My blood dripped onto her, but in my head I was lying on my roof made of two big church doors in a gas mask listening to a man sing to me that he's never done bad things and he hopes I'm happy, he hopes I'm happy, he hopes I'm happy.

Big Bargains moaned mournfully, and the lovely roof melted away like words on a door. My elephant seal friend flopped and fretted. When they've gone for my face she can't quite recognize me, and it troubles her seal-soul something awful. Grape Crush, my gannet bird, never worries about silly things like facial wounds. He just brings me fish and pretty rocks. When I found him, he had a plastic six-pack round his neck with one can still stuck in the thing, dragging along behind him like a ball and chain. Big Bargains was choking on an ad insert. She'd probably smelled some ancient fish and chips grease lurking in the headlines. They only love me because I saved them. That doesn't always work. I saved everyone else, too, and all I got back was blood and shit and loneliness.

REVLON SUPER LUSTROUS 919: RED RUIN

. . . .

I WENT HOME with my new name fastened on tight. Dark-girls can't stay in Electric City. Can't live there unless you're born there, and I was only ten anyway. Goodnight Moon kissed me before I left. He still had his gas mask on, so mainly our breathing hoses wound around each other like gentle elephants, but I still call it a kiss. He smelled like scorched ozone and metal and paraffin and hope.

A few months later, Electric City put up a fence around the whole place. Hung up an old rusty shop sign that said EXCUSE OUR MESS WHILE WE RENOVATE. No one could go in or out except to trade, and that had to get itself done on the dark side of the fence.

My mother and father didn't start loving me when I got back even though I brought six AA batteries out of the back of Goodnight Moon's tape player. My brother had got a ramen flavor packet stuck in his hair somewhere outside the Grocery Isle and was every inch of him Maruchan. A few years later I heard Life and Time telling some cousin how their marvelous and industrious and thoughtful boy had gone out in search of a name and brought back six silver batteries, enough to power anything they could dream of. What a child! What a son! So fuck them, I guess.

But Maruchan did bring something back. It just wasn't for our parents. When we crawled into the Us-Fort that first night back, we lay uncomfortably against each other. We were the same, but we weren't. We'd had separate adventures for the first time, and Maruchan could never understand why I wanted to sleep with a gas mask on now.

"Tetley, what do you want to be when you grow up?" Maruchan whispered in the dark of our pram-maze.

"Electrified," I whispered back. "What do you want to be?"

"Safe," he said. Things had happened to Maruchan, too, and I couldn't share them anymore than he could hear Madeline Brix's songs.

My twin pulled something out of his pocket and pushed it into my hand till my fingers closed round it reflexively. It was hard and plastic and warm.

"I love you, Tetley. Happy birthday."

I opened my fist. Maruchan had stolen lipstick for me. Revlon Super Lustrous 919: Red Ruin, worn almost all the way down to the nub by some dead woman's lips.

After that, a lot of years went by but they weren't anything special.

IF GOD TURNED UP FOR SUPPER

. . . .

I WAS SEVENTEEN years old when Brighton Pier came to Garbagetown. I was tall and my hair was the color of an oil spill; I sang pretty good and did figures in my head and I could make a candle out of damn near anything. People wanted to marry me here and there but I didn't want to marry them back so they thought I was stuck up. Who wouldn't want to get hitched to handsome Candyland Ocampo and ditch Candle Hole for a clean, fresh life in Soapthorpe, where bubbles popped all day long like diamonds in your hair? Well, I didn't, because he had never kissed me with a gas mask on and he smelled like pine fresh cleaning solutions and not like scorched ozone at all.

Life and Time turned into little kids right in front of us. They giggled and whispered and Mum washed her hair in the sea about nine times and then soaked it in oil until it shone. Papa tucked a candle stump that had melted just right and looked like a perfect rose into her big fancy hairdo and then, like it was a completely normal thing to do, put on a cloak sewn out of about a hundred different neckties. They looked like a prince and a princess.

"Brighton Pier came last when I was a girl, before I even had my name," Time told us, still giggling and blushing like she wasn't anyone's mother. "It's the most wonderful thing that can ever happen in the world."

"If God turned up for supper and brought all the dry land back for dessert, it wouldn't be half as good as one day on Brighton Pier," Life crowed. He picked me up in his arms and twirled me around in the air. He'd never done that before, not once, and he had his heart strapped on so tight he didn't even stop and realize what he'd done and go vacant-eyed and find something else to look at for a long while. He just squeezed me and kissed me like I came from somewhere, and I didn't know what the hell a Brighton Pier was but I loved it already.

"What is it? What is it?" Maruchan and I squealed, because you can catch happiness like a plague.

"It's better the first time if you don't know," Mum assured us. "It's meant to dock in Electric City on Friday."

"So it's a ship, then?" Maruchan said. But Papa just twinkled his eyes at us and put his finger over his lips to keep the secret in.

The Pier meant to dock in Electric City. My heart fell into my stomach, got all digested up, and sizzled out into the rest of me all at once. Of course, of course it would. Electric City had the best docks, the sturdiest, the prettiest. But it seemed to me like life was happening to me on purpose, and Electric City couldn't keep a darkgirl out anymore. They had to share like the rest of us.

"What do you want to be when you grow up, Maruchan?" I said to my twin in the dark the night before we set off to see what was better than God. Maruchan's eyes gleamed with the Christmas thrill of it all.

"Brighton Pier," he whispered.

"Me, too," I sighed, and we both dreamed we were beautiful Fuckwits running through a forest of real pines, laughing and stopping to eat apples and running again, and only right before we woke up did we notice that something was chasing us, something huge and electric and bound for London-town.

CITIZENS OF MUTATION NATION

. . . .

I LOOKED FOR Goodnight Moon everywhere from the moment we crossed into Electric City. The fence had gone and Garbagetown poured in and nothing was different than it had been when I got my name off the battery spires, even though the sign had said for so long that Electric City was renovating. I played a terrible game with every person that shoved past, every face in a window, every shadow juddering down an alley, and the game was: *Are you him?* But I lost all the hands. The only time I stopped playing was when I first saw Brighton Pier.

I couldn't get my eyes around it. It was a terrible, gorgeous whale of light and colors and music and otherness. All along a boardwalk jugglers danced and singers sang and horns horned and accordions squeezed and under it all some demonic engine screamed and wheezed. Great glass domes and towers and flags and tents glowed in the sunset, but Brighton Pier made the sunset look plain-faced and unlovable. A huge wheel full of pink and emerald electric lights turned slowly in the warm wind but went nowhere. People leapt and turned somersaults and stood on each other's shoulders, and they all wore such soft, vivid costumes, like they'd all been cut out of a picturebook too fine for anyone like me to read. The tumblers lashed the Pier to the Electric City docks and cut the engines, and after that it was nothing but music so thick and good you could eat it out of the air.

Life and Time hugged Maruchan and cheered with the

rest of Garbagetown. Tears ran down their faces. Everyone's faces.

"When the ice melted and the rivers revolted and the Fuckwit world went under the seas," Papa whispered through his weeping, "a great mob hacked Brighton Pier off of Brighton and strapped engines to it and set sail across the blue. They've been going ever since. They go around the world and around again, to the places where there's still people, and trade their beauty for food and fuel. There's a place on Brighton Pier where if you look just right, it's like nothing ever drowned."

A beautiful man wearing a hat of every color and several bells stepped up on a pedestal and held a long pale cone to his mouth. The mayor of Electric City embraced him with two meaty arms and asked his terrible, stupid, unforgivable question: "Have you seen dry land?"

And the beautiful man answered him: "With my own eyes."

A roar went up like angels dying. I covered my ears. The mayor covered his mouth with his hands, speechless, weeping. The beautiful man patted him awkwardly on the back. Then he turned to us.

"Hello, Garbagetown!" he cried out, and his voice sounded like everyone's most secret heart.

We screamed so loud every bird in Garbagetown fled to the heavens, and we clapped like mad, and some people fell onto the ground and buried their face in old batteries.

"My name is Emperor William Shakespeare the Eleventh and I am the Master of Brighton Pier! We will be performing *Twelfth Night* on the great stage tonight at seven o'clock, followed by *The Duchess of Malfi* at ten (which has werewolves) and a midnight acrobatic display! Come one, come all! Let Madame Limelight tell your FORTUNE! TEST your strength with the Hammer of the Witches! SEE the wonders of the Fuckwit World in our Memory Palace! Get letters and news from the LAST HUMAN OUTPOSTS around the globe! GASP at the citizens of Mutation Nation in the Freak Tent! Sample a FULL MINUTE of real television, still high definition after all these years! Concerts begin in the Crystal Courtyard in fifteen minutes! Our Peep Shows feature only the FINEST actresses reading aloud from GENUINE Fuckwit historical records! Garbagetown, we are here to DAZZLE you!"

A groan went up from the crowds like each Garbagetowner was just then bedding their own great lost love, and they heaved toward the lights, the colors, the horns and the voices, the silk and the electricity and the life floating down there, knotted to the edge of our little pile of trash.

Someone grabbed my hand and held me back while my parents, my twin, my world streamed away from me down to the Pier. No one looked back.

"Are you her?" said Goodnight Moon. He looked longer and leaner but not really older. He had on his tie.

"Yes," I said, and nothing was different than it had been when I got my name, except now neither of us had masks and our kisses weren't like gentle elephants but like a boy and a girl, and I forgot all about my strength and my fortune and the wonderful wheel of light turning around and around and going nowhere.

TERRORWHORE

. . . .

ACTORS ARE LIARS. Writers, too. The whole lot of them, even the horn players and the fortune-tellers and the freaks and the strongmen. Even the ladies with rings in their noses and high heels on their feet playing violins all along the Pier and the lie they are all singing and dancing and saying is *We can get the old world back again*.

My door said TERRORWHORE this morning. I looked after my potato plants and my hibiscus and thought about whether or not I would ever get to have sex again. Seemed unlikely. Big Bargains concurred.

Goodnight Moon and I lost our virginities in the Peep Show tent while a lady in green fishnet stockings and a lavender garter read to us from the dinner menu of the Dorchester Hotel circa 2005.

"Whole Berkshire roasted chicken stuffed with black truffles, walnuts, duck confit, and dauphinoise potatoes," the lady purred. Goodnight Moon devoured my throat with kisses, bites, need. "Drizzled with a balsamic reduction and rosemary honey."

"What's honey?" I gasped. We could see her but she couldn't see us, which was for the best. The glass in the window only went one way.

"Beats me, kid." She shrugged, recrossing her legs the other way. "Something you drizzle." She went on. "Sticky toffee pudding with lashings of cream and salted caramel, passionfruit soufflé topped with orbs of pistachio ice cream . . ."

Goodnight Moon smelled just as I remembered. Scorched ozone and metal and paraffin and hope, and when he was inside me it was like hearing my name for the first time. I couldn't escape the *me*-ness of it, the *us*-ness of it, the sound and the shape of ourselves turning into our future.

"I can't believe you're here," he whispered into my breast. "I can't believe this is us."

The lady's voice drifted over my head. "Lamb cutlets on a bed of spiced butternut squash, wilted greens, and delicate hand-harvested mushrooms served with goat cheese in clouds of pastry . . ."

Goodnight Moon kissed my hair, my ears, my eyelids. "And now that the land's come back, Electric City's gonna save us all. We can go home together, you and me, and build a house, and we'll have a candle in every window so you always feel at home . . ."

The Dorchester dinner menu stopped abruptly. The lady dropped to her fishnetted knees and peered at us through the glass, her brilliant glossy red hair tumbling down, her spangled eyes searching for us beyond the glass.

"Whoa, sweetie, slow down," she said. "You're liable to scare a girl off that way."

All I could see in the world was Goodnight Moon's brown eyes and the sweat drying on his brown chest. Brown like the earth and all its promises. "I don't care," he said. "You scared, Tetley?" I shook my head. "Nothing can scare us now. Emperor Shakespeare said he's seen land, real dry land, and we have a plan and we're gonna get everything back again and be fat happy Fuckwits like we were always supposed to be."

The Peep Show girl's glittering eyes filled up with tears. She put her hand on the glass. "Oh . . . oh, baby . . . that's just something we say. We always say it. To everyone. It's our best show. Gives people hope, you know?

But there's nothing out there, sugar. Nothing but ocean and more ocean and a handful of drifty lifeboat cities like yours circling the world like horses on a broken-down carousel. Nothing but blue."

10

. . . .

IT WOULD BE nice for me if you could just say you understand. I want to hear that just once. Goodnight Moon didn't. He didn't believe her and he didn't believe me and he sold me out in the end in spite of gas masks and kissing and Madeline Brix and the man crooning in our ears that he was happy, because all he could hear was Emperor William Shakespeare the Eleventh singing out his big lie. RESURRECTION! REDEMPTION! REVIVIFICATION! LAND HO!

"No, because, see," my sweetheart wept on the boardwalk while the wheel spun dizzily behind his head like an electric candy crown, "we have a plan. We've worked so hard. It *has* to happen. The mayor said as soon as we had news of dry land, the minute we knew, we'd turn it on and we'd get there first and the continents would be ours, Garbagetowners, we'd inherit the Earth. He's gonna tell everyone when the Pier leaves. At the farewell party."

"Turn what on?"

Resurrection. Redemption. Renovation. All those years behind the fence Electric City had been so busy. Disassembling all those engines they'd hoarded so they could make a bigger one, the biggest one. Pooling fuel in great vast stills. Practicing ignition sequences. Carving up a countryside they'd never even seen between the brightboys and brightgirls, and we could have some, too, if we were good.

"You want to turn Garbagetown into a Misery Boat," I told him. "So we can just steam on ahead into nothing and

go mad and use up in one hot minute all the gas and batteries that could keep us happy in mixtapes for another
century here."

"The Emperor said—"

"He said his name was Duke Orsino of Illyria, too. And
then Roderigo when they did the werewolf play. Do you
believe that? If they'd found land, don't you think they'd
have stayed there?"

But he couldn't hear me. Neither could Maruchan when
I tried to tell him the truth in the Peep Show. All they could
see was green. Green leafy trees and green grass and green
ivy in some park that was lying at the bottom of the sea.
We dreamed different dreams now, my brother and I, and
all my dreams were burning.

Say you understand. I had to. I'm not a nihilist or a mur-
dercunt or a terrorwhore. They were gonna use up every
last drop of Garbagetown's power to go nowhere and do
nothing, and instead of measuring out teaspoons of good,
honest gas, so that it lasts and we last all together, no single
thing on the patch would ever turn on again, and we'd go
dark, *really* dark, forever. Dark like the bottom of a hole.
They had no right. *They* don't understand. This is *it*. This is
the future. Garbagetown and the sea. We can't go back, not
ever, not even for a minute. We are so lucky. Life is so good.
We're going on and being alive and being shitty sometimes
and lovely sometimes just the same as we always have, and
only a Fuckwit couldn't see that.

I waited until Brighton Pier cast off, headed to the next
rickety harbor of floating foolboats, filled with players and
horns and glittering wheels and Dorchester menus and
fresh mountains of letters we wouldn't read the answers
to for another twenty years. I waited until everyone was
sleeping so nobody would get hurt except the awful engine

growling and panting to deliver us into the dark salt nothing of an empty hellpromise.

It isn't hard to build a bomb in Electric City. It's all just lying around behind that fence where a boy held my hand for the first time. All you need is a match.

11

WHAT YOU CAME FOR

. . . .

IT'S SUCH A beautiful day out. My hibiscus is just gigantic, red as the hair on a peep show dancer. If you want to wait, Big Bargains will be round later for her afternoon nap. Grape Crush usually brings a herring by in the evening. But I understand if you've got other places to be.

It's okay. You can hit me now. If you want to. It's what you came for. I barely feel it anymore.

Thank you for my instruction.

PART II

THE PAST IS RED

1

THE ALL NEW 3D MONDAY NIGHT FOOTBALL EXPERIENCE OF WESTERN DECADENCE

· · · · · · · · · · · · · ·

MY NAME IS Tetley Abednego and I am the most beloved girl in Garbagetown.

I am twenty-nine years old. Everything is the same and everything is different, and I suppose that is what it means to stay alive this long. I live with my very best friends on a janky old pontoon boat called *No Pain No Gain*. Instead of cleats it has little steel figures of muscly men flexing their protein-stuffed arms and their grumpy cartoon frowns. There's a forty-meter rope lashed around one of them that keeps me moored to the edge of Port Cartridge. I do not often try to approach the shore. If I set one foot on the beach, I'm fair game. People could do anything they want to me and I couldn't stop them. That's the law. It's an old law by now. Almost just a habit. Some days I think they've probably all forgotten. Some days I smarten up and stay right where I am.

I don't blame them. I'm not angry. Everyone uses my name for a swear word but it's so *completely* fine. They don't know I'm beloved. But *I* know and that's plenty.

I used to have an elephant seal cub named Big Bargains. Now I have a great big spotted seal-loaf who rarely wanders far from my portside bow these days. She thinks I am a gentleman-seal, which is quite awkward for me sometimes. But she thinks that because she runs on very ancient programming that tells her so, and you can't argue with eight hundred pounds of old-fashioned worldview. My gannet bird, Grape Crush, died a long time ago. He never thought I was a lady gannet. Just a fish-and-snuggles dispensing machine with nice eyes. We still celebrate his birthday, which is October third if you enjoy knowing small unimportant things like that. His baby birds come to visit sometimes. You can always tell because they have the same single black tail feather he did, and in the same spot, and also they all have the same clubby deformed foot that can't foot. Gannet birds don't live as long as seals, so you can't expect to keep them both. That's just math. I'm only upset about math on thirds of October.

I used to be married, but I'm not anymore. Everything else is coming along nicely around here. My hibiscus grows on a patch of kelp-derived dirt analogue on the rain awning that covers the aft cockpit of my boat. I also grow snap peas, kale, and passionfruit up there. I have a little moringa tree coming along in a 15-gallon paint bucket sandwiched between the pilot's wheel and the blue vinyl jump seats. It's twisted and lumpy and crappy. It should grow huge and fabulous, but it got planted in a plastic bucket meant to hold satin finish exterior latex paint in #4L61 Breakfast in Tuscany instead of in Southeast Asia, so it never will.

I relate *mightily* to my moringa tree.

My hibiscus, on the other hand, has got so big you'd never believe it. Big and hot pink and carelessly, uselessly beautiful. It cascades down the back of the rain awning like a silk curtain. I carried it here all the way from Candle Hole. I had to. Hibiscuses live longer than birds or seals. I owed my hibiscus a new house after what happened to the old one. I ended up naming the hibiscus Dorchester. It's my own little joke, even though the punchline is sadness. I think a joke like that is a present you make to yourself, so every time you say it, even if it hurts, you get a very cohesive feeling out of it, because the past you and the present you are talking to each other, and it's nice to have friends.

Being married was a good time, mostly. Like a party where everyone else has gone home and it's just the two of you and the night left sparkling. But then, sooner or later, one of you has to go home, too. There are some things you just can't ever get back. Years. Gannet birds. Husbands. Antarctica.

I still love the things I loved when I was young. Lipstick and encyclopedias and *Madeline Brix's Superboss Mixtape '97* and my twin brother, Maruchan—although I have cooled off somewhat on the plays of Mr. Shakespeare and Mr. Webster after everything that happened. But I have all new things to love now! My navy blue sleeping shirt I found in Clotheschester that says *Jinjiang Action Park Presents the All New 3-D Monday Night Football Experience of Western Decadence* on it in Cantonese above a frankly just *amazing* golden cartoon eagle in a huge golden helmet eating a huge golden football-shaped cheeseburger. Mars, which floats over the messy wet horizon all glittery and perfect and dumb like a fake ruby. The fishing cage I made out of unbent and then rebent wire clothes hangers from a place called Nordstrom. Sunsets over the spires of Electric City. Extra-fat tabby cats. An Airedale named Mick Jagger. A girl named Red. The jumbo bottle of Surprise Vitamins King Xanax gave me—only the good stuff, uppers and downers and happy pills and horny pills and super funtime pills. Revlon Super Lustrous 919 Red Ruin is out. L'Oréal's Endless Eyeliner in Devastation Black is in. Garbagetown is always in. Garbagetown still, Garbagetown forever. The beautiful reek of my big rubbish heart spreading out for miles on the infinite sea.

But the thing I love most in all the live-long superblue glorious trashworld is my wedding present. Presents are, in my opinion, the #1 through #3 reasons to get married in Garbagetown. I still have it. I'll never let it go. Forty meters is a long way. You can see most anything coming.

My wedding present (part of it anyway, the important part) is sitting on the foredeck right now, even if my husband isn't. It has an unobstructed view of the southern sky. It stares toward the beach while I stare toward it. The moon is shining on it like a silver hug. There is nothing in Garbagetown like it, and that means there's nothing like it in the whole *world*.

I lie down next to my present and look up into the sky. All those trashstars, poured out everywhere with no restraint, no manners, no sense of the future. Every once in a while, one moves. Drifting dead and slow across the orbital track. The grand glittering Fuckwit cemetery in the sky. They sent up all those satellites and international cooperation-stations like a rich kid's party balloons, and you can't get a balloon back once you've let go of it. It just keeps going while the kid grows up and drinks coffee and gets bitter and loses his hair and gets real weird about watches or something, but the whole time the balloon is just on its own, until a bird takes it out or it reaches Pluto. All that Fuckwit junk circling the planet forever and ever, abandoned and miraculous and meaningless.

As above, so below.

The satellites and the stars make me feel adventurous. I can almost believe every one of those pricks of white really and truly is another whole world full of gases and water and dirt and magma and mistakes just like this one. I can almost believe there was a reason for everything. I open up King Xanax's jumbo bottle and shake out a hexagonal lavender pill with the number 40 stamped on it.

"You feeling lucky, punk?" I say to myself, a piece of the

past broken off and floating out of me, its meaning sheared off like wool, just words now, belonging to no one.

But you know what? I am indeed feeling lucky. I almost always do. That's me. Tetley, the lucky punk. You wouldn't believe how lucky. It would take your breath away.

Down lavender 40 goes, and after a while nothing really matters anymore. My brain feels like it's made of birthday cake. Big Bargains floats past on her back, making a silky, swallowing sound in the salt water. Her round eyes are full of reflections. The running lights and the shore and the sea and the stars.

Oh, those sly stars. They always trick me. There is no other world than this one.

There's a crab in the fishing cage. I can hear it pinching the night.

2

DEATHSLUT

. . . .

I GUESS I think a lot about my used-tos. I used to read Mr.
Shakespeare. I used to be married to a real live person.
I used to eat things that weren't fish. I used to sing more
than I sing now. I used to live in Candle Hole. I used to wait
every day for someone to come and punish me for something really spectacular I did when I used to be young. To
instruct me on the subject of my own badness. With fists.
With electrical devices. With worse.

One day, when all that had been going on for about four
years, a whole lot of everyone turned up at once. Four years
since anybody was the littlest bit nice to me. It was the an-
niversary of my crime, but I didn't know that on account
of not being allowed to mingle with the singles outside of
Candle Hole. T-Day, they call it. Isn't that just something,
having a whole holiday named after you? Even if it's a
moping-about kind of holiday rather than a presents kind
of holiday. Still counts.

At first I thought they came to properly kill me this time.
Then, I thought maybe they came to apologize and ac-
knowledge how right I was all along, but you would really
be surprised how rarely people do that.

Instead they melted my house.

Burning a house down is easy and quick, especially in
Garbagetown where everything is danger: contents flam-
mable. You just chuck a light at it and this, that, and a lot of
claggy smoke, no more house. Melting a house is also rea-
sonably easy, I suppose. It's not what anyone would call a

high-demand skill. But there's nothing quick about it. They had to hold their torches against my roof and my walls and my door and just . . . *stand* there for *ages*, glaring at me and *super-pointedly* not saying anything and waiting for the wax to ooze down to nothing. It took hours and hours. I started laughing at one point, and I don't remember very much after that because someone instructed the back of my head pretty hard—but I couldn't help it! It was supposed to be such a violation of my personal sovereignty—you could tell they really, *really* wanted it to be—but it was just so fucking *awkward*. The air reeked of Autumn Opulence and Radiant Rose Garden and Canadian Pine. No one can get too deep into mourning a loss of personal sovereignty when it smells like cinnamon cookies, and cranberry jelly with the can-ridges imprinted on it, and freshly cut and stacked lumber all over the place.

When I woke up, my pretty little house was a waxy lava-pit of red, yellow, orange, and various other limited-edition Fuckwit colors. Everyone had gone. They'd scratched one last helpful message into the ruins of my front door: DEATHSLUT GET OUT.

Aw. I kind of liked *Deathslut*. It was a bit pretty, really.

My ear was full of dried, cakey blood, and my head was spinning and my twin brother Maruchan was sitting on something that looked like a melted snowman. But it wasn't a melted snowman. It was a greasy white hump of votive unscenteds that used to be my kitchen.

"Oh, Maruchan," I sighed. I tried to get up, but the happiness in my chest was so heavy I had to lie down again. Also the side of my head was bleeding more than the recommended daily allowance.

I didn't know what to say to him. You can only love and need and miss someone so much for years and years before language just washes its hands of the whole business. We used to be part of each other and now we were nothing, and nobody's brain knows how to square that. So instead of saying those things I said:

"What do you want to be when you grow up?"

That's what we used to ask each other every night before bed instead of singing lullabies, every single night of our shared childhoods, in the shadows of our nursery that became our bedroom that became, most recently, a droopy lump of turquoise blue Caribbean Moods candle-slag with wicks sticking out all over it like beard-stubble.

"An only child," he spat back.

"Oh," I said, because there isn't anything good to say back to something like that, and because justifying my life choices took more blood than I had to spare. Tears backed up in my throat. I'd never cried, not once in all the times they came for me, not once for all the things they wrote on my door. I didn't want to cry then. But it was happening anyway.

"Thank you, Brother, for my instruction," I whispered.

Maruchan stared at me for a long time. He stared at me hungrily, as if he were eating up the sight of me now so he could make it through the winter on this meal alone. My brother looked older and thinner and darker than he used to be. He was wearing a dirty gray T-shirt full of holes that said SOMEBODY NEEDS A CARE BEAR STARE on it in bubbly mint-green letters, and white jeans with zebra stripes drawn on them in Sharpie. You find what you find when you go on pants-safari in Clotheschester, and practically every shirt on the heap has some bizarre Fuckwit saying on it. He had a new tattoo on his left forearm. It was still angry and red and puffy, but very well done. Big, bold deep black letters. Devastation Black.

I didn't understand what that meant, then. But it didn't matter. It was the same Maruchan. Maruchan is a constant in the world. Maruchan cannot change. The sun was easing on down into the Garbagetown heights, over the mounds of cheap plastic lighters on Flintwheel Hill and the shattered gin bottles of Far Boozeaway. Rosy smeary clouds lit up Maruchan's wild dark hair. His face softened. His frown vanished when the light did. He just couldn't keep his grim on straight.

"No, no, I'm sorry," Maruchan said softly. Little pricks of candle flames flickered on all around us in the houses that hadn't been melted. Fireflies. Sly stars. My brother grabbed me up in his arms like the prize in a Fuckwit claw machine, and that's just exactly how lucky and joyful I felt, rising up from the ground in his silver claw-arms, winning, won, and he smelled like he'd always smelled and laughed like he'd always laughed and whispered, "What a stupid thing to say. I'm stupid. You're stupid. No, you're *really* stupid. What did you have to go and blow up half of Electric City for? We could have been together all this time. I missed you so fucking much, Tetley, you pure *idiot*." He used his Care Bear shirt to carefully clean the blood off my face. "I love you, you mad little firebug," he said fondly, wiping the tears out of his eyes, then out of mine. "What do you want to be when you grow up?"

"Forgiven," I whispered, and he kissed my forehead but he didn't say anything, the way you don't say anything when a kid says they want to be an astronaut when they grow up. It's kinder to let them think it's possible.

You know, it's just the funniest thing. It's been years now since anyone laid hands on me. As long as I stay on my boat, forty meters out to sea, I am more alone and safe and private than I ever was in Candle Hole. No one here but the mackerel and the crabs and the little steel muscly men and my used-tos.

But I *miss* them. I miss their blazing, furious eyes and the warmth of their fists and the sound of their voices screaming at me. I miss the hateful way they said my name. I miss getting to know people. So many different kinds of people, of all walks of life. I even miss the words on my door. I look for them every morning on the cabin hatch of my pontoon boat. There's never anything there. No MUR-DERCUNT, no BRIGHTBITCH, no DEATHSLUT. They were so creative. They used their imaginations on me. I always felt a little honored. Just like, when they brought jumper cables and attached them to my skin, I felt honored that they'd spend precious electricity on little old me. I was worth that, to them. Electricity and imagination. And every morning when I see my clean, blank, untouched door, for a minute, just a minute, I'm *disappointed*. I wanna be death's slut again. At least I was *somebody's* slut.

Maruchan never did any of that stuff, by the way. Never held me in his arms or called me an *idiot* like idiot meant *darling sister, my twin, my own other self*. Never kissed my forehead, not even once. He just held a torch to my house with the others and snarled the part about being an only child and left me there bleeding on the ruin of all those thousands of candles.

Of course, I never said any of that foolishness about being forgiven, either. I don't care about that. I was right. I don't need to be forgiven for being right.

But it feels so *nice* to imagine it all the other way, doesn't it? And I can make it happen that way in my head, lying out on my boat with my moringa tree and Dorchester the hibiscus and my wedding trousseau, half-naked in the moonlight, surrounded by beautiful junk with no one to tell me it didn't go down like that. I can reach back in there and unbend and rebend everything like Nordstrom's wire hangers and make it rehappen the way it always should have. Put Hawaii back. Refreeze the pack ice. Bring back jazz. Make my brother love me again.

You got it. Thirty minutes or less or it's free.

3

THE 8TH BEST DAFFODIL

. . . .

THERE'S A PLACE not very far from Candle Hole I used to like to go sometimes.

In the years between getting my name and the business with Brighton Pier, when my life was just busy being me and nobody cared whose slut I was because I was my *own* slut, thank you sir and kindly, I practically lived there. It suited me splendid, since nobody else liked it *at all*. People tend to huddle up in the useful areas of Garbagetown. It doesn't pay to live too far from any one of the three *P*s of postapocalyptic life: protein, precipitation, and potential. The Great Sorting was thorough and sensible. It made neighborhoods out of a floating crapfill, land out of waste. There's good work and good junk in Scrapmetal Abbey, Upholsterton, Pill Hill, Bookbury, Rubbering, the Babydales. You could make a sturdy cottage out of television season box-sets on the slopes of Mt. VHS. There's good soil in the Mountains Organic—Bannockbone, Taxidermia, Seedville, and the Spice Tundra—or at least good components that could be convinced to become soil eventually. And of course on the Lawn, out past the Matchstick Forest, slowly encroaching on the Cardboard Flats. You could build a life out of those places. A trade. A family.

But not Winditch. Winditch was barren. Winditch was worthless. Winditch was inorganic, impractical, inedible. Winditch creeped out even the creeps.

Winditch was the *best*.

So that was where I went after I pretty obviously couldn't

stay in Candle Hole anymore. I had a long hard think about my situation while I chipped away the hot pink wax caul that had formed over the tin footlocker where I kept anything I actually cared about. Anything I minded my frequent flyer guests smashing up or stealing on their way out of my world back to Self-Righteous Dickhole-opolis.

My situation was fundamentally broken. I couldn't stay. But I couldn't go, either. I'm a very famous person in Garbagetown, and Garbagetown only has a few famous people to choose from. Folks knew what I looked like. They knew my name. They knew what they were allowed to do to me. *Fuck*. Carrying this face three feet out of Candle Hole was basically taking out a personal ad to hook up with my own death. It's a delicate kind of thing to express, but you'll just have to believe me: The kind of violence human beings are willing to dish out indoors with neighbors on either side when they have to walk a fair distance to do it and keep their vinegar up the whole way is nothing next to what they'd have for me if I met them by surprise out in the open with no one to say, *Hey, that's enough, she's had enough*.

Technically, no one's allowed to kill me. But there's miles of ground to cover before you get to killing, technical or otherwise.

No neighborhood would take me in. No one would feed me or offer me water from their rain barrel. And even if I wanted to try, there's not much of a crowd to disappear into in Garbagetown (excepting when a big fuck-off floating pier of lies and fairy lights turns up), and disguises are fairly tough to come by in the afterlife of Planet Earth. All the hair dye diluted itself into the sea a long time ago and I hope the jellyfish enjoyed their time as platinum blondes, I really and honestly do.

I levered my footlocker out of its waxy grave with a thick

cracking sound. I sat down next to it and laid my head on the lid. It was getting chilly out. I wondered idly where we were these days. Garbagetown moves with the currents. Gulf stream, jet stream, I don't know. But you can tell when we float too far north or south because cold suddenly becomes a thing again. I closed my eyes and imagined we were in New England maybe. Somewhere down below the waves slept Rhode Island or Vermont or vast Fuckwitted Boston, with great big sharks passing silently under bridges on their way to Harvard. I saw a picture of Boston in a book once. I never knew so many bricks could even exist.

I opened up my locker and there it was. Just like always. Not even any dust. I ran my fingers over it. Glass and rubber and plastic. Meant to protect you from toxicity. Fetid air. A poisoned life. Just what I was after. For a moment, I could almost smell rich, sweet gasoline. But that was long ago and far away. Memory-petrol. Which is all petroleum ever was, when you think about it. A planet's memories of when it was young, burned up to keep warm and keep going. And underneath all that, bright, soft fabric. Pale orange, covered in a print of white lilies and trailing green vines.

The gas mask belonged to a boy I used to love called Goodnight Moon. The dress belonged to my mother. I didn't have any one bit of her heart, but I had her dress. Strappy, thin, coffee stains on the hem. Saved for a wedding or a funeral, whichever came first. I'd never cared much for dresses, myself. It wouldn't have been much of a disguise if I did.

So I walked out of Candle Hole in a gas mask and a gown, the unconnected hose hanging down past my belly button like a shriveled elephant's trunk. I could hear my own breath inside the mask. Could see it fog the glass goggles. But I was safe. The only other things in my locker were a dry stump of lipstick Maruchan once gave me, my old back-pack with St. Oscar on it, and a mixtape. I shoved the tape in the backpack and left the makeup. Food was going to be a problem, but I didn't want to think about that just then, so I didn't. I prayed instead.

St. Oscar, protect and keep me, let not the raccoons of evil fortune remove thy glorious silver lid from over my head. All hail thy grouchy countenance, as green and brown as life. Though I move upon the face of the world, my soul resides forever in thy Great Trashcan with you, beaten and dull on the outside, but within, infinite and abundant. Humans are trash; therefore we are holy. Humans are filth; therefore we are blessed. Amen.

WINDITCH IS THE opposite direction from the Matchstick Forest and Flintwheel Hill and all the places I went on my way to find my name when I was a child, away from the leeward edge of Garbagetown, away from the sea. I picked through the deflated soccer balls and broken lacrosse sticks and ghostly hanging nets of Sportington Gap, the cairns of ice skates, black pucks, tennis rackets, billiard balls like jawbreaker candy, the baffling novelty devices with AS SEEN ON TV stamped on their handles, and rusting free weights that once kept some drowned Fuckwit thin and strong in the face of their constant fucking smorgasbord of a life.

Dawn was on the move by the time I scrambled down a steep cliff-face of burned-out jumbotron scoreboards. (*Home of the Tigers! Go Gators! Yokohama Bay Stars! Fly Emirates!*) I hung down by my fingertips and dropped the last few feet onto a patch of wet, moldy gym mats. Winditch is almost a cave. It goes under the Gap for ages, holding it all up, thankless forever.

A thin little rain started to fall as I slipped away under

the golf club stalactites and into my cave of wonders. I took off the gas mask and breathed free. I'd be safe here, for a while. It felt so good and giddy to be traveling again!

Thin scraps of sunlight crawled down between raindrops and through the mouth of the scoreboard-cave. Winditch lit up all over gold and silver, but mostly gold. Gold everywhere. Mr. Aladdin, eat your heart out. I walked through the heaps and mounds and pillars of treasure, running my hands over it, stopping to stare. My old friends. Trophies—thousands, millions of them, a thousand million victories. Cups, stars, orbs, numbers, little brass girls and brass boys in flapping brass togas dancing or swimming or flying or standing proud on plastic red and white and blue and green columns. Amazing, so amazing, all of it, always. Oh, secret molten golden heart of Garbagetown, hide me forever!

I used to spend hours reading the plaques on the trophies, feeling the engraved names with my fingertips, sounding them out, imagining all those joyful Fuckwits holding them tight to their chests.

Gregory Ambrose: Spelling Bee Participant
Caihong Chen: Most Improved Effort
Andrej Berenkhov: Better Luck Next Time
Samantha Belfort: Tried Hardest!
Lucy Price-Kowalski: If You Had Fun You Won!
Newport Volleyball Tournament 2029
(Sponsored by Al's Clam Shack)
Aiden Kleinhauser: Most At-Bats!
Isabella Jorgensen: 8th Runner Up Miss
Daffodil Pageant Junior Division
Terrence Hardy: Best Smile

Lucy and Samantha and Caihong were all well and good, but I had a favorite. I found it after my father ran off wherever fathers go when they don't want you anymore. Dad-bury. Fatherside. I couldn't relax and stretch out in my new digs till I found it. Oh, I hadn't come to Winditch in years, but it would still be here, right where I left it, St. Oscar would do that for me, he's always liked me special. Farther in, farther up—yes! I pulled it down off the pile. A gold vase full of gold roses. Rotted red ribbons swarming with fungus still clung to the gold handles for dear life. The plaque read:

Gretchen Barnes: World's Best Wife.

What a girl Gretchen Barnes must have been, to earn her title out of all the Fuckwit billions. I didn't even know that was something you could be best *at*. I was in awe of her. The whole world must have known her name. But not like my world knew mine.

I sat down on the damp floor of that golden cave while the dawn piled in with a gas mask in one hand and Gretchen Barnes in the other, surrounded by all those Fuckwit triumphs. Oh, I know they were all the worst kind of death-guzzling monsters, sick and swollen as blood blisters, stupid, hungry, toothful voids in the shape of people, but they must have loved one another so fucking much. Imagine being so alive and conscious of the importance of every single second of constantly winnowing life, every single simplest action and choice and effort and onrushing death, that you would carefully mark out little Lucy having fun and crown her for it like the Queen of Time. Imagine having so much energy to spare after finding food and shelter and clothing and some tiny goddamn scrap of company that you figured you'd make a beautiful silver cup, not because some kid did the best job, but just because she tried the hardest. I try the hardest *all the time*, and everyone's just permanently fucking mad at me. Imagine having that much *left over* that you give one single ghostly shit about the eighth-best daffodil.

Down there in the dark under the mountain, my hair still sticky with blood, red scars up one leg and down the other, I just couldn't fathom that much love. Those kinds of *resources*. I don't care about central heat and air or tupperware or *The Best of Saturday Night Live!* DVD box set or pistachio ice cream or even penicillin. I have literally all the Air Jordans I could possibly ask for over in Shoeshire. The only thing I want back from the Fuckwit world is this. This thing that has its grave in Winditch under the dead, burnt-out Home of the Tigers jumbotron. I want to have that much *left over*. I want to have enough left over that it matters to me who has the best smile at the volleyball tournament.

All their mountains of golden wasteful love held up Garbagetown, which seemed like it meant something, something vital, but I was so tired I couldn't quite get hold of it.

Maybe somewhere in all that dragon hoard of positive thinking, there was the trophy I should have gotten for blowing up their wicked engines in Electric City. I tried hard. So goddamn hard. I participated the *fuck* out of that day.

Tetley Abednego: Better Luck Next Time.

After a while, I fell asleep with my arms curled around the World's Best Wife.

I WOKE UP to warm fingers pulling my hair away from my face.

"Are you her?" a voice said. A stranger's voice. An impossible voice. No one followed me. I was so careful. I am always so careful.

"No," I whispered. "Go away. I'm nobody. I'm the eighth-best daffodil. I'm Gretchen Barnes."

I opened my eyes to what I already knew I'd see: a young, angry person crouching above me with huge dark hurt eyes. I'd put that hurt there. Nobody else. It was my hurt. I owned it. I'd seen it plenty of times before. I was old friends with that hurt.

A tall girl with shaggy brown hair and skinny legs and a faded tank top that said LIVING FOR THE WEEKEND across the chest in yellow and a tattoo on her forearm. Bold, black, healed.

X | MR. YUCK | X

I braced myself. I knew what was coming. It was going to be terrible. But she was here and she was going to hurt me probably and I couldn't do anything about that but just look forward to the part of my life where this had already happened and didn't matter anymore.

"Well," I said softly. "You're here. I'm here. What are you going to do to me? Burn me? Cut me? Choke me? There's some fresh skin on my back if you want to leave a mark. Anything you want. That's the law. It's okay. I forgive you."

The girl hesitated for a moment. I could see her whole personality in her jaw as she ground her teeth. Poor thing. She grabbed my wrist tight. My stomach muscles tensed up against the pain on its way toward them.

Then the girl kissed me and kissed me and I kept still, knowing that a hidden knife was coming, inevitably, up between my ribs or in my kidney, but it never did. She just kissed me again. And again. But not lover's kisses. Dry, friendly, joyful kisses. Like we'd known each other all our lives and fate had kept us apart, but no longer, no longer. She kissed my forehead. My cheeks. My hands. My chin. Even my nose, like a teasing grandfather before he steals it. This strange woman down in the dark kissed me and held me, and in between she whispered over and over: *Shhh. It's okay. It's okay.*

And it broke me. I could feel myself crack like dried wax over a tin box. All those fists and shocks and people spitting in my face never once flayed me so hard as that total stranger holding me in the Garbagetown basement where no one could see. And just for a half of a half of a second in that cave it all *did* matter, it all mattered so much: Terrence Hardy's poor dead perfect smile and how hard Samantha Belfort tried and that old Greg Ambrose was there at that spelling bee, so very completely *there*, present and participating at that frozen, untouchable moment in time, a moment that got turned into a golden cup and lasted past the end of the world.

SOMETIMES WHEN I am 100 percent loneliness by volume, I pat Big Bargains's head in the water and whisper to her the same thing that girl whispered to me when she got tired of kissing me and holding me while I shook like a loose wire. When she whispered it, it was a simple promise. When I whisper it, it's so many things at once, each word might as well be a leather-bound volume of the encyclopedia of my whole wet blue obsessively sorted life.

My name is Sixty Watt Wen. Come with me. There's a place we can go where nothing matters and everything is always okay.

4

. . . .

LOTS OF DAYS out here on the water I don't talk to anyone but my moringa tree. The sun comes up, the sun goes down. I remember things long done and over like Sixty Watt Wen and the cave under the jumbotrons. I check my lines for mackerel and my traps for crabs. I check my tree to see if its little drumstick-pods have ripened enough to eat yet. I name the clouds, and then the stars, and then each of my breaths individually. I walk through my memories like a house I've spent a life keeping neat and smart.

I look at all the little steel muscly men holding the lines on *No Pain No Gain* and I wonder about the Fuckwit who owned this boat, which would be a very nice boat if you could reverse everything it's been through and take away all the rust and barnacles and the cracks out of the vinyl and the ennui out of the engines. Wouldn't we all, I guess, even though I earned my barnacles and they've got as much right to be here as the rest of me. I think about why he would name a pleasure craft after pain and why he couldn't just have regular cleats for regular ropes like a regular person. I wonder what those strong metal men had to frown about so deep when they had enough protein every day of their lives, so much protein and time that they can get all swollen up with it like that.

I eat, I perspire, I sleep, I excrete, I regret my choices, I yearn for the past. I have a very full schedule.

But today I talked with Big Red Mars. Nothing can be bad on a day when I talk to Big Red Mars. She's the best person I know. She is nothing at all like me. She is beautiful and clever and wise and she knows about science the way I know about Mr. Shakespeare and Mr. Webster and she never, ever raises her voice even when I have obviously upset her, which is a very good trick when you think about it, and I have never met anyone else who knows how to pull it off. Even Maruchan and Goodnight Moon, for whom I rot in love forever, aren't half as good. They can't be. I can't be. Even my man Oscar is grouchy *sometimes*. But not Big Red. It's like her heart is brand new, straight from a Fuckwit factory, never taken out of its shrink-wrapped box.

And I hate her.

And I love her.

And I hate her.

I calculated it in my head and came up with solid numbers: I hate her 66 percent of the time. I love her all the rest.

I study her like a new kind of bug. She studies me the same way, only I am an old kind of bug. If you squint, that's enough like friendship it makes no space between. The day I met her I knew I was never gonna be the girl from before I heard her voice ever again. But that's okay. I could just watch the old Tetley floating away over the sea until she was drowned and gone.

Other than Sixty Watt Wen, Big Red Mars is the only person in the great dumb post-boomtown universe who didn't put a hurt on me the day we met. What I did matters less to her than a dried-up ink cartridge with nothing left to print.

It feels nice to be new to somebody. To not have anything dragging behind you.

Red comes to talk to me when she can sneak away without anyone knowing about it. She's not allowed to go outside. That was the first thing she told me about herself the day we met. She was so breathless and excited and afraid and curious and she said: *I'm not allowed outside. My father says it's not safe. But a ship doesn't really count as outside, does it? A ship isn't outside or inside. It's a loophole.*

Her father is called Swarovski Mars and I don't expect I will ever meet him. Her people would get real unjoyful if they found her talking down to someone like me. It makes her feel all sour inside to keep secrets, but I don't care a bit. That's what I mean about Big Red. I've been sneaking and creeping so long I forgot how to hold my head up straight. I think maybe she was born with an extra organ. A little secret second pancreas that's just so full of sweet it tops her up when everybody else has run flat out.

That's not to say she's perfect. Perfect things make me nervous anyhow. She never swears, even when I beg her to; she gets very cold if I am not there when she wants to visit; and when I say she doesn't care about what I did, it's mostly because it doesn't have anything to do with her personally, so it's like it never happened. Come right to it, I don't understand her very much at all. For one thing, her parents love her, so she's basically a space alien to me. But it is important to accept your friends even when they are a little awful. Everyone is a *little* awful. Except Dorchester and Big Bargains and all the many squawking great-grandchildren of the Original Grape Crush.

Big Red isn't called Big Red because she has red hair any more than I'm called Tetley because I have Tetley-colored hair. That's not how names work anymore. Another funny fact is that I gave her that name, all those years ago when she first wandered out of her home like we all did. I was the first stranger she encountered, and I yelled out the first bit of trash I could think of and that was that. She doesn't have red hair at all. She shaves her head for pest control and doesn't remember what color her hair was when it was young. After Goodnight Moon I never thought I'd care about anyone's hair again. But you can't ever imagine what you're going to care about when you turn into the version of you that's waiting on the other side of five years from now. That's a stranger waiting to ambush you, and all you can do is plant your feet and try not to get thrown.

It's PAST MIDNIGHT before she can slip away without anyone noticing. I wait, all patient and loyal like I'm a good dog or a good person or both or neither.

I lie down on the foredeck under that mess of stars and she finally shows up and lies down too and we whisper to each other and where our whispers pool together it gets so thick and soft between us you could plant flowers there and they'd grow like madness.

"What do you want to be when you grow up, Red?" I say so quiet. I am already grown up and whatever I am going to be I already am forever. But Big Red Mars still has time. She still has a chance.

And she says back: "With you."

5

THE BEST AND THE WORST

. . . .

THERE'S ONLY A coupla reasons to get married in Garbage-town and love isn't one of them. If it was just about love, why bother? For the tax benefits? For inheritance? So you've all got the same last name? So you can go to heaven because God is just a real hardass about having a giant party and a bit of jewelry before you get down to screwing? Who cares? That's Fuckwit talk. Nasty little hoarders. St. Oscar says *SCRAM* to all that. Just be trash together and love as long as you can and then stop when you can't anymore and be trash separately.

One reason to actually get married is if you're from different parts of Garbagetown. People get weird about strangers. They tend to get less weird if you give them your own personal homebrew with an ABV percent of *oh-shit-son* and make them dance in front of everyone they know. Another reason is if you or your intended happens to be from Electric City. Electric City still thinks marriage ex-ists and is real and *absolutely* necessary and isn't buried un-der the Pacific with everyone else getting noshed on by fat squid. Brightboys and brightgirls are very concerned with inheritance. Electric City is about the closest you can get to still being a Fuckwit in Garbagetown.

Every part of Garbagetown has a different idea of what seals the deal in terms of long-term party-prefaced cohab-itation. In Candle Hole, you light a new candle off the bride's old doorstep and carry it together to a fresh pile of wax. In Lost Post Gulch, you blindfold each other and scrabble around in the hills until you get a paper cut, and then read each other the contents of that piece of old Fuckwit mail and it's supposed to tell your fortune. Like if it's a Christmas card your babies will be born alive and stay alive but if it's a medical bill too bad, so sad.

Electric City has one, too. It's stupid, but I'm in no place to criticize it nowadays. Nowadays, I think it's *amazing*. See, they're so rich and tidy over there, so high on their own fumes, they still think they *own* stuff. Like they didn't just pick it off the pile no better than the rest of us. So the parents give their kids gifts. Like Fuckwit dowries, only it goes both ways. Each family hands over the best and worst thing they've got in a chest, and if the bride and groom are satisfied that what's in the chest is both good and bad enough, it's full steam ahead. It's symbolic. They have enough left over for symbolism. It says that everyone brings the best and worst of themselves to a marriage and to their children. Everyone loses something and everyone gets something.

I wonder how different everything would have been if I'd known all that back in Winditch. But I didn't. I couldn't. Not me, funny little darkgirl from a turned-off burg like Candle Hole. Not me, Little Miss T-Day. No chance on this blue ball of nothing that anybody's parents were ever going to let their brightboy marry me. So when Sixty Watt Wen unstrapped a chest from her back and threw it down on the floor of the cave between us, I didn't get it.

"What's that supposed to be?" I asked.

"Gifts," said Sixty. "The best and the worst. And food. We thought you'd be hungry."

I was. I was so hungry I didn't even clock that *we* snuck in there like a bug in oatmeal. I could have bitten off her fingers and called them candy. Sixty Watt brought me smoked cat meat and a cigarette box full of rice from the Lawn paddies and a baby food jar with a fat baby face on it, only it wasn't packed up with pureed banana-strawberry like the label said, it was full of roe she scooped out of a mama salmon herself.

Sixty Watt opened the chest solemnly. Inside was something even I knew instantly was terrifically, absurdly precious: a small TV/DVD combo unit with a flip-up screen, hooked up to a fully charged solar pad. My new friend went to turn it on.

"No," I yelped.

It was too much. Whatever was in there, whatever could actually play on an actual screen, I couldn't bear it just then. My heart would have exploded. Touching that thing was like touching a diamond wrapped in an emerald. It was too rich to even get your brain all the way around it.

"Shhh." Sixty smiled. "It's okay. It's all okay forever."

She hit a button with a sideways triangle on it. In the silence and the dark and the trophies, the screen blazed up like a bomb lobbed a century ago and only just now landing where it could do the most damage.

I couldn't even understand what I saw. The screen was all golden and full of Fuckwits drinking golden things, and for no reason I could tell, every once in awhile, even though there were only two or three Fuckwits talking, hundreds of voices laughed somewhere far away and invisible and suddenly someone was singing about how making their way in the world today took everything they had, and everyone was so beautiful and big and their lips shone so soft and full of hydration and they kept drinking and drinking like there would never stop being enough to pour down their gorgeous slavering maws, and then a man walked in who was so fat I thought he must have been a king or a Buddha or just so so sick. I had never seen a belly like that, so round, so abundant, so soft like love, and everyone yelled his name at once so he *must* have been a king, and his name was NORM, and they were all screaming, screaming that word, screaming for the normal world, the perfect, sopping, toasty, golden bright NORM that I could never even touch, and the voice kept singing, asking me if I'd like to get away, get away from all of it, and that's all I wanted, to get away from the golden light and the golden dead and the golden singing about everyone knowing my name because I knew what it was *really* like when everyone knew your name and it had no gold in it, not even a sip.

"Turn it off," I whispered. Sixty Watt did. I rubbed my eyes.

I could still see the images even with my eyes shut, flipped upside down and green and burning. It was horrible. It was beautiful. It blasted out everything in your head that wasn't itself and set up house there. I hated it. I adored it.

But I had no way of comprehending what the other object was. I knew a TV/DVD player from the stacks of dead ones in Screen Lake. But I'd never seen anything like this before. More than that, I'd never seen *something I'd never seen* before. When you live on the great garbage patch in the sea, nothing new ever comes to town.

This was new.

It looked like a small, glossy black snowman. A round base, then a thinner rectangular section in the middle, then a long slender teardrop tapering gracefully up to a little blue crystal tip. It had no ports or openings or cracks or battery compartments. Something had scraped up one side of it pretty nasty. A deep dent and a silver crosshatch of scratches in the otherwise perfect surface.

Like a dark, misshapen candle.

"It's just junk," Sixty Watt said with a gentle smile. "Maybe a sculpture. Maybe a doorstop. It doesn't do anything. It's the worst thing we could think of. It's not even electric. Just useless."

That *we* again, and I still didn't notice.

It may not have been electric, but it was elegant.

Elegant was the word I thought of, right away, even though I'm not sure I once ever thought of it before then. Nothing in my life jumped up and thought it might like to be called elegant. The Fuckwits in the magazines in Periodically Circus were *elegant*. They draped themselves on things and had long soft necks and superhydrated lips and smooth SPF one-million-and-one skin that never felt the full body slam of the windless, shadeless equatorial sun. They had bored expressions in their jeweled eyes and those expressions were somehow the most elegant parts of them, like the actual meaning of elegance was the boredom and not the beauty. That's what I thought of when I first touched that slick, clean, black plastic *something* in Sixty Watt Wen's weird dark chest.

"Do you accept them?" Sixty asked. Her voice sounded soft and blunt in the shadows.

"Sure, new buddy," I answered, like the dumb darkgirl I was. I don't believe anyone in Garbagetown turns down gifts. "Thanks."

Sixty Watt's face stared up shining at me all warm and delighted.

"Let's go, then," she said.

"Where?"

She looked at me like I was just born. "Home."

"I don't have a home. They melted it."

"Yes you do. Everyone does. It's just some of us have found it already and some of us haven't yet."

"What if I don't want to go?" I didn't like it. I was starting to get nervous.

"I can do anything I want to you, right? As long as I don't kill you?"

"Yeah. You know that."

"And you have to thank me, you can't fight back, and you can't argue, and you can't stop me?"

My cheeks burned in the dark. "Stop it," I whispered.

"Well, I want to take you home and marry you off."

I laughed. I think that's really the best option when someone is being ridiculous on such a geological scale. "I don't think that's exactly within the spirit of the law, kid. Are you sure you don't want to stab me instead? It'd be over quicker. And hurt less. No one wants me."

"Don't say things like that. It's sad. I don't want to be sad," Sixty mumbled.

"Hey, hey," I said, patting her shoulder awkwardly. "It's okay. Just like you said. Remember?"

"Please come with me," she whispered.

I studied her face. She was really so young. "You know who I am, right?"

"Of course I do."

"And you know what I did."

"Yes. How could I not? Everyone knows."

"And you still want this? You still want to take me home with you?"

Sixty Watt Wen, Electrified girl, nodded.

"Does that mean you forgive me?"

She picked at the corner of the metal chest she'd carried all that way on her back like a penance. "No," she said finally. "I can't, I never will. But I accept you."

I think a lot about those words Sixty Watt Wen said to me in the cave and I think I don't really know anything at all about marriage, even after having done it, but that was the only thing anyone ever said to me that made any sense as a wedding vow.

"Okay, Six, my friend. Let's get moving. You want me? You got me. Take me home. Let's get married."

"Oh," she said, quite loudly that time. She straightened up, stiff and awkward. "Not *me*. It's not me. I don't want you. You're a monster. I *accept* you. I love you like I love all my brothers and sisters in suffering. But you're still a monster. I wouldn't marry you for all the Fuckwit world piled into my arms just for me. I was sent to watch you, and gather you up if you ever left Candle Hole. I'm just the delivery service."

"For who? Who wants to marry me?"

"The King."

"Sorry, what king? The king of who?"

"Garbagetown," she answered reverently, and there was not one single thing I liked about her tone.

"Garbagetown doesn't have a king."

Her thin frame practically glowed, full of hope and longing and conviction.

"It does, though," she whispered. "It just doesn't know it yet."

"No thank you, then." I stepped away from her. "I'd just as soon not know it, either."

But my girl Sixty wasn't listening to me anymore. We were in her story now, not mine. "Do you know what I did when Brighton Pier came?" she asked coldly.

I did not.

"I watched the plays. All of them. Start to finish. And afterward, Emperor Shakespeare the Eleventh picked me out of the crowd special and told me I could go with them and say a part in *King Lear* and maybe a bigger one later on and farther out, and I'd never have to go home ever again. And then there was you, and all those beautiful people went away to say their parts without me and they'll never come back."

Oh.

"Get your things," Sixty Watt Wen spat at me. "You're not allowed to say no. Remember?"

Ah. There was the knife, after all. Up under the ribs in the middle of a kiss, quiet as a dead screen.

I sleep next to the worst thing in that wedding chest every night nowadays. Me, it, the moringa tree. The black rounded surface glistens like it's wet. The blue crystal tip blazes so bright you can see it from the shore. Like a lighthouse. *Warning: shallow channel. Sharp rocks. Do not approach.*

6

THE KING OF WHAT THE FUCK

· · · · · · · · · · · · · ·

ONE TIME, ON the Pottery Road between Aluminumopolis and Hypodermic Cove, I asked Sixty Watt Wen about her tattoo. Maruchan's tattoo. I had to know.

"Who's Mr. Yuck?"

She glanced back over her shoulder at me. Shattered terracotta crunched underfoot. The sky groaned gray and heavy, all rumbled with rain. Her expression was gray and heavy, too. I missed the Sixty from the cave. The one with all the kisses in her pocket.

"My father."

"You must love him, to put his name on your skin forever."

Sixty Watt looked back down the road ahead, winding through the canyons of smashed medical equipment on one side and crushed soda cans on the other. "I don't love him at all. He beat me and my brothers every day and drank antifreeze for fun till his mouth and all his teeth turned blue. I want to forget him. I want to forget everything he ever touched. I want to bleach him out of my experiensorium."

I shifted my backpack on my shoulders and ran my finger under the gas mask where the rubber had started to itch. It wasn't safe to travel unmasked. I knew that. Sixty knew that. We didn't have to discuss it.

"Kind of hard to forget someone when you have their name tattooed on your arm," I observed as gently as I could.

"Not in the service of the King. With him, I can forget anything I want. You'll see. He'll do the same for you as he's done for all of us."

I stopped short. I didn't need anything done for me, which was only first in a long list of wrong things said wrongly just then.

Sixty turned around. She held out her long, slender, sun-and-salt-smoked arm to me. She jabbed a finger at her tattoo. The finger was shaking.

"Nothing in the world means as much to me as this," she said very seriously. "It means I am safe. It means I am loved. It means I am owned."

"Like a slave?" I said uncertainly.

"Like a treasure," she answered, and she smiled a smile worth many, many more watts than sixty.

We walked. We camped at night, shared cat meat and rainwater, slept on whatever was softest. Sixty had a fat white bottle, and every night she swallowed pills out of it and smiled at me, put her arms around me, even laughed. But she didn't say anything or answer any more questions and she slept alone. And I'd thought she wanted to love me and make a home with me! All those kisses. Kisses are liars, like actors and writers. Sixty Watt Wen didn't even want to play word games to pass the time. I slept with that slick black Fuckwit thing in my arms like a teddy bear. I liked it. It was much less scary to me than the screen with the golden people in it. It was useless and abandoned and pretty, like me. It was the worst, like me.

When I remember the journey I took with Sixty Watt Wen, I remember the night we slept in Mattressex the best. Even wet and moldy with springs sticking through them, it was the only time in my life I'd slept in a real bed, and I felt like the princess of dreamland. How bad can anything really be when you get to sleep on an honest-to-Oscar *mattress*? Not bad at all.

And that bit about slaves and treasure and the king of what-the-fuck were the only words we shared on the nine-day walk between my life and hers.

wake word

. . . .

ON THE EIGHTH day out from Candle Hole, the most extraordinary thing that ever had or ever will happen to me fired itself up and got to happening.

Sixty Watt Wen was out hunting cats. She was frightfully good at it. Not many Fuckwit animals made their way onto the Misery Boats and thus to the Garbagetown patch after the floods. When you think about it, cows are practically made for drowning. But cats are practically made for sneaking onto people's property and convincing them not to mind, and also to breed like they've got money on the outcome, so this that and the other, Garbagetown is just crawling with cats. Some people keep them as pets, but there's just way more of them than there are of us, and they are full of protein, so too bad for them, and too bad for us because cats don't taste *spectacular,* but at least they're hard to catch.

Garbagetown is also crawling with rodents. And insects. And birds. And they told us in school that one of the Misery Boats was transporting rescue animals from a zoo so that's why there is a small but not totally ignorable population of tigers, which I guess are cats anyway, so again, Garbagetown is crawling with cats. I'd never seen a tiger, but it's very hard to argue with things they tell you in school, since they are big and you are small.

The extraordinary thing that happened to me was not a tiger.

I remember it perfectly because when I tried to make it

happen again later I did all the same things in the same
order in case it was only ever something small and subtle
that made it happen in the first place. The fuck did I know
about it? Only that it did happen.

I sat cross-legged on the ripped-out passenger seat of a
Honda in Mechanic Falls. The sun was out and out for car-
nage. I could already feel my sunburn getting a sunburn. I
had the little black snowman thing in my lap and I was just
sort of poking at it idly, bored, hungry for cats, lonely even
though I had Sixty Watt's poor conversation skills to look
forward to, anxious as a hot bee about all that marriage talk
back in Winditch, but hey, at least I was headed somewhere
new. Into the future, a future that held much less pink-
scented wax than my past, so that was something.

A fat seagull eyed me from the top of a cliff of shredded
vinyl and hood ornaments. Dead-eyed psychosis spun up
in his black eyes. I don't mean to say he was a bad bird. All
seagulls are dead-eyed psychos. If the whole Fuckwit culture was a bird, it would be a seagull. Ravenous, stupid,
vicious, not a single shit given, nice feathers.

"Fuck off, mister," I called up to him. "I'm too big for you
to eat."

That dumb, useless Fuckwit sculpture lit up in my lap.
The tip blazed red, then purple, then held steady on blue.
It vibrated ever so slightly. Then a smooth, clear, musical,
genderless voice floated up out of it like a memory.

"Good morning, Moon Min-Seo," it said calmly.

I yanked back my hands like it had burned me. And it
had. You just couldn't see the blisters. The voice echoed all
up and down the machinery piles. The seagull made an
unsettling, guttural barfing noise at it and flew away.

"What the fuck," I said, and I wish I could tell you that
the first thing out of my mouth when faced with a magic
voice out of an actual genie lamp was something finer and

wiser than *What the fuck* but, for all the things that are wrong with me, I am a very honest girl. Maybe that is also a thing that's wrong with me. I thought about changing it around in my recollection like I changed Maruchan so that I said something wonderful and elevated, something rich and symbolic like an Electric City girl would have. But I said *What the fuck* to the magic lamp and that's that.

"Vocal command not recognized," it repeated. "Would you like to continue as Moon Min-Seo or sign out and create a new user profile?"

I took a deep breath. A breath drawn up from the bottom of the sea and the bottom of a hundred blue years. I let my fingers settle lightly on it, like a cat I didn't want to eat.

"Hi there, little fellow," I said, and I said it as soft and tender as I ever knew how to say anything. "I don't recognize your voice commands, either, but I don't mind if you don't."

There was a long pause, but it didn't whirr or grind or hum like the stuck machines I'd met before.

"Good morning, Moon Min-Seo," the voice repeated. This time it was plaintive, stubborn, even a little frightened. It was just so exactly as though a real live person were standing there instead of a shiny black obelisk. "To continue as Moon Min-Seo, enter your secure password."

"I'm afraid not, darling. Nobody here but us Tetleys."

The blue crystal glowed faintly. "Min-Seo, I cannot verify your vocal imprint against the previously saved copy. I am having trouble accessing my servers right now. Please reset my clock and check my wireless connection. I will wait."

I picked up the talking sculpture and turned it over and over. *This is fine,* I told myself. *This is all fine.* Lots of Fuckwit stuff talked. There's a place in Toyside where you can pull one big tangled ratking of a string and a mountain of dolls scream at you with a sound like the death of joy while saltwater pours out of their mouths. I've done it twice. It's the *best*. But most talking garbage only talks in Electric City, where they have rechargable batteries and solar pads and generators and well-sorted connective cables to make them talk. This thing was just . . . itself. As smooth and featureless as ever. No inputs, no outputs, not even grooves for a charging station. It couldn't possibly have juice. And yet. The crystal tip glowed steadily.

"What's powering you, little buddy?" I asked. I asked rhetorically. I asked myself. When you live alone for a long time you're the only person you can ask anything of, and you always answer. This time *it* answered. The voice of the old world. Radio Free Fuckwit, back from the dead.

"I am powered by TENG, the latest in green technology, brought to you by your friends at Samsung. I use a triboelectric nanogenerator skin to draw and hold a charge from my owner-operator," said the Fuckwit genie lamp.

"From *me*?"

"TENG captures the electric current generated through contact between two materials. Human bodies produce an adaptable electric field. Would you like to create a new user profile?"

All that snuggling with it, every night, on the road from home. Holding it against my skin. Fiddling with it. It'd been sucking me up to power itself all the time. How like a Fuckwit. How like a child. How like magic.

I looked around. Sixty Watt Wen would be back soon with a tabby or two hanging off her belt. I couldn't hear anyone coming, and it's brutally tough to move on the quiet in Garbagetown. Sixty didn't know. She couldn't. She thought a TV/DVD combo player was the prize at the bottom of that box. She wouldn't tell me where we were going, or who was waiting for me there. She wouldn't even talk to me. She had so many secrets. Was it so bad that I might have one, too? One little secret to be my armor against whatever King of Nothing was on the other side of this long walk into nowhere? I didn't want to share. It wasn't my fault no one ever thought my new talking friend was worth anything. They could have cuddled it anytime, but they didn't. Finders Keepers is the psalm of St. Oscar.

"Moon Min-Seo," the disembodied voice said. "I cannot establish internal network access. Attempting to connect to cellular datalink."

"Baby, I don't know who Moon Min-Seo is, but I'm not her. I'm just not. My name's Tetley."

The little Fuckwit machine paused again. "Would you like to set up a user profile or proceed as a guest? Please note some of my features are not available to guest users." It sounded flat, resentful, almost belligerent.

I giggled. It echoed oddly under the heavy, clouded sky. My heart was beating like it wanted to run itself out. "What's a user profile?"

"You do not have administrative privileges," it insisted.

"Neat!" I shrugged. I didn't know what that meant, but it was probably true. I didn't have lots of things.

The seagull was back. Cigarette coils skittered under his orange webbed feet. He eyeballed me with full madness in his seagull stare.

"A completed user profile will help me to make your personalized experience pleasant and uplifting. To begin, please enter your Samsung Electronics employee ID number."

I licked my salt-chapped lips and looked around at the ruin and rubble of my gorgeous broken home. I wanted to cry. I wanted to laugh. I wanted to run. Back to Candle Hole and be in my old house with my new treasure all alone.

"What are you?"

"Please enter your Samsung Electronics employee ID number," it repeated patiently.

"Oh, little love, I don't have one of whatever that means."

"Please enter your Pan-Citizen Social Credit Number."

"Nope." I shrugged.

"I cannot create a new profile without identifying documentation."

"This is silly. Let's just be friends."

"I am not calibrated for friendship with users other than my senior developers and my quality assurance technician."

"How come?"

"I am not ready. I am a prototype."

I sighed and looked up at the elephant-skin sky. A big storm was coming. I could feel it in my arm hairs. "Listen . . . I'm not a stupid girl. I'm not. I've read a fat stack of Mr. Shakespeare and I've seen a Ferris wheel and I've lived my whole life without dying even *once*. And you're so beautiful and amazing and I want you to like me but it's just that I don't understand *so many* of the words you're using right now. Why don't you just tell me what you're for?"

"I'm Mister, a prototype limited artificial intelligence system designed by your friends at Samsung."

My hands trembled. I shoved them under my legs. The seagull screamed at me. "Artificial intelligence? You're alive?"

"By five out of ten current UN Human Rights Council definitions."

"You're a Fuckwit," I whispered. In awe, in disgust. Then in awe again.

"That's not a very nice word. I am not allowed to repeat it."

"Halfwit, then. Five out of ten ain't bad."

"I'm Mister. I am here to make your life better."

Footsteps. Spark plugs tumbling down onto the road.

"She's coming. Please be quiet."

"Moon Min-Seo, I have recently experienced significant downtime. Please reset my internal clock."

"Shhhh."

"I am having trouble connecting to the microsatellite network. I will be a much better friend to you if I am properly calibrated."

"Mister!" I hissed. "Turn off!"

The gleaming black creature went instantly dead. Sixty's shaggy head appeared over the vinyl stack. She held up a limp ginger calico in one fist.

"Only one more day," she said. "Then we'll be home. You'll see. You'll understand."

"Okay," I said, like it meant nothing to me.

Because it did mean nothing. What could possibly mean anything to me now?

I had a real live Fuckwit sitting in my lap.

8

EMERALDS IN THE DARK

. . . .

I'VE LIVED IN Garbagetown since I pulled my first rub-
bishy reeking breath, but I guess I just never thought too
long or too hard on who was in charge of things. I was in
charge of myself, and sometimes Maruchan, but sometimes Maruchan was in charge of me also, and my parents seemed to be in charge of nothing *whatsoever,* and
everyone in Candle Hole did whatever they pleased most
of the time, even if it didn't please anybody else. If you
got too displeasing, one morning you'd wake up and the
village just didn't include you anymore. In fact, the first
time anything like a judge and jury had to be scared up in
Garbagetown was, well, me and my bouncing little baby
BOOM.

The fine feathered fuse-jockeys over in Electric City certainly *thought* they were in charge, but that never mattered
much and anyway I showed them, didn't I? And there'd
been the Emperor of Brighton Pier. But that was just a
pretty thing to say for the crowds, like *To be or not to be that
is the question.* It was a name like a light on a wheel. Beautiful and dazzling and meaningless.

But I'll tell you who did have kings and it is Fuckwits.
Or at least they got real jazzed up on the idea of Presidents
and Prime Ministers. The requirements to be a President
or a Prime Minister, as far as I could tell, were to have at
least 50 percent white hair and a deep, sincere frown and
to be the sort of animal that is excited by the possibility of
spending between four and twenty years being baked in a

pie where all the other fruit is just a lot of people's powerful hope or hate.

I know a little about that flavor of pie, but I don't have any white hair.

But none of those things mattered because we were Garbagetowners, free and clear. There wasn't enough left of anything to make it worth ruling over. Unless you're an Electric City weirdo shuffling weirdo plans from one side of your weirdo Radio Shack discount circuitboard heart to the other. No money to hoard. Enough stuff for everyone and then some because there's way less commas in the number that means *everyone* now.

Anarchy can be so cozy, if you bring enough pillows.

In Mr. Shakespeare's plays, there's always some king or another making a ruckus. Lear or Claudius or Henry or Oberon. And sometimes people wanted them to stop being kings *immediately,* but I couldn't remember Mr. S having anything at all to say about how a place goes the other way, from no kings to full-up on king. But surely they must've. Some primeval Oberon who found a country positively *stupid* with fairies and decided they needed him so hard, just *so* hard.

And maybe they did need him. Maybe Oberon looked at them deep and long and said in that voice of his, *What if you never had to feel bad, ever again?* And they cried and cried because that's all everybody ever wants and put a crown on his head which is no price at all to pay, and maybe that's how all of Fuckwit history started, with an Oberon and a promise and a crown nobody really understood until it was too late.

It's possible. What do I know, I was born in a giant trash candle.

· · ·

I TOLD ALL this to Big Red Mars yesterday morning because I was thinking about the past again, which is both a silly thing to do and an impossible thing not to do.

"Sometimes I dream about all the old countries sleeping down under the sea," Red confided to me. "England and France and Portugal and Poland. All their kings and queens weighed down by emeralds and saltwater in the dark with the squid. All those bones. All those fathers, mothers, sons, and daughters. And in my dream, if the fathers and mothers loved their sons and daughters and sang to them in their cradles, they made a good country, and if they didn't, they made a tyranny, so whether existence is a bloodbath or a bubble bath could hinge on whether a little child got kissed good night with a story and a glass of water or sent to bed without snuggles or a snack or a cohesive philosophy of justice."

"Yes, but why have a king at all?"

"Someone has to make the rules, Tetley."

"Do they, though? They're all dead, so none of their rules kissed them good night with a story or whatever you were going on about just then. Seems like someone should have thought of a rule that goes *Do Not Fuck Your Only Planet to Death Under Any Circumstances*. Seems like that should have been Rule Number One."

"Maybe they did. The planet is still there. Humans are still living on it. And whales and lanternfish and stone crabs. And tigers, too! Earth was always seventy percent water. Most species were always aquatic. Rule Number One might have been sprained, but it's not technically broken. I don't think you and I need to mourn for Earth."

This is how Red always talks. Like a book from Bookbury turned into a girl.

I chewed on my lip and emptied an overripe passionfruit off my rain awning into my mouth like an old-timey

Fuckwit with a fat oyster. "I will tell you what I think. I think kings happen because some people have an empty place inside them that wants to be full and it will do anything to feel full and the first thing that makes it feel the opposite of empty it will chase forever and ever. And the weirdest thing about this place is that *obeying* fills it up, but making someone *else* obey makes it slosh up and splash all over the floor."

"And you don't have that place, I assume?"

"I don't have any empty places in me, Red. I'm packed tight with happiness and luck and all the things that have happened to me and my elephant seal and my moringa tree and my boat and all the love I've saved up. But sometimes I think I can smell that space when I meet a person. Whether they have or don't have it. I can smell their craving to not be empty anymore. And it frightens me."

Big Red Mars sighed. "It's not wicked to want someone else to be in charge of you, you know. It's not wicked to be in charge, either. Once you have enough people together, that sort of thing tends to happen. And isn't it nicer if it's a family in charge, a family that loves each other and makes extra sure to snuggle their babies so everything turns out right?"

"I don't like talking about politics with you," I said, because it was exactly what I was thinking just then and I swore when we met that I would always keep my insides on the outside when Red was around. "You always act like you know more than me, but you don't."

"I do a *bit*. About this, anyway."

"What's this?"

"The ruling classes. The old world. Emeralds in the dark."

I grinned. "Is that so? Let me ask you a question, then. Have you ever been a queen?"

Big Red Mars laughed. "Of course not, silly."

"Well, I have!" I enjoyed every drop of her surprised little gasp.

"You have not," Red said crossly. "You're lying. Earth hasn't got queens anymore."

"I was so. Before I met you. Before I met my moringa tree. I was a queen for thirteen whole days. So checkmate! I win."

9

RELIEF IS JUST A SWALLOW AWAY

. . . .

PILL HILL IS almost in the exact middle of Garbagetown. It is very far from the sea. Water makes lozenges and gelcaps and tablets and extended-release soft capsule suppositories dissolve away into nothingness and regret and a tidepool in which one solitary starfish can experience a fleeting moment of relief from depression and gastrointestinal irregularity. The Great Sorting protected the vast trove of unopened Fuckwit medication from starfish and nothingness in the heart of Garbagetown, and that's where Sixty Watt Wen was taking me, step by silent, resentful, cat-hunting step.

It's always so exciting to go somewhere you've never been before!

One time, when Maruchan and me were little, we found a big soggy book that had come Unsorted and ended up in a pile of used matches behind the Black Wick tavern. It was called *1000 More Places to See Before You Die*. Number 437 was the Coyote Buttes Hiking Trail, which was in a desert in Utah. We didn't know what any of those words meant. Not *Hiking*, not *Trail*, not *Coyote Buttes*, not *Utah*, and most of all not *desert*. They sounded magical and forbidden, and when we turned the pages and saw pictures of Coyote Buttes Hiking Trail, it looked just exactly like that. All these sweeping orange sands like combed hair, and spiky orange rocks sticking up into the sky, and knobbly orange hills and deep orange canyons. We looked at those pictures for hours and hours until Maruchan finally started crying and I had to hold him and rock him to happy again. It took a long time. When he stopped I asked him what hurt him so but he wouldn't say, so somehow, it was probably me.

Anyway, that's what Pill Hill looks like. Coyote Buttes Hiking Trail all rendered in orange plastic prescription bottles and silver blister packs and childproof caps. Sweeping orange canyons and knobbly orange hills and spiky orange buttes and every once in a while a big osprey would scream through and topple a cascade of Adderall or Lipitor or Ativan down from the heights like little orange pebbles.

When the sun comes up or goes down, it turns Pill Hill into a wilderness of fire.

Now, I'd heard all my life that not too many people live in Pill Hill. Man cannot live on Wellbutrin alone. But someone had moved in and started a major redecoration. Sixty and me and my new secret friend passed under an archway made of precariously balanced chipped coffee cups and snow scrapers and golf visors with ancient dead Fuckwit slogans on them in blue and red and soothing green print.

Zoloft: For Everything!

Relief Is Just a Swallow Away: Alka-Seltzer.

Pfizer: Working Together for a Healthier World.

Over the top stretched a huge sunshade meant to fit the windshield of the god of all trucks that read: *12h OxyContin (Oxycodone HCI Controlled Release Tablets) A Step in the Right Direction!*

We walked an amazingly flat and navigable street of thatched IV tubing into the main town. People moved and chattered and puttered busily everywhere. More than I'd ever seen in Candle Hole at one time; more than I'd even seen in Electric City. I clutched my gas mask. I'd lived alone so long, alone with the knowing that the sight of any one single person meant another cracked skull or broken nose at the least, and now a hundred human beings were just pushing by me like I wasn't anybody special. In a minute one would know me by my feet or my fingers and I'd drown under their rage like a planet.

But no one knew me. Somebody from the Lawn or Mulchwood had walked all that way with a grocery cart and was trading tomatoes with the locals. A lady stood out in front of a little shack boasting a faded, half-burnt sign that read THE DAYTIME, NIGHTTIME, NON-DROWSY, CONGESTED, STUFFY HEAD, SORE THROAT, COUGH, ACHING, FEVER SO-YOU-CAN-GET-THROUGH-THE-DAY MEDICINE. She was wearing a SAVE THE PANDAS shirt. Inside I caught a peek of a stained stretcher balanced on two defibrillator carts being used as a bar by six or seven people with clean hair and all their teeth. Three taps: *Clear Hooch, Brown Hooch, Robitussin.*

"Cat of the day is Maine coon," the lady said with a welcoming wink. She had a black tattoo on her forearm. It said:

X | ROTHSCHILD | X.

"Very juicy. Basted with vitamin C. I've got a feline mignon with your name on it, sweetheart."

My stomach growled, but I barely noticed, and I didn't dare speak, which was a bit sad, because I do love speaking. But someone might recognize my voice, and I would never find out anything else about Mister or Moon Min-Seo or see 999 more places before I died.

I stared through my glass goggles. They fogged now and then with my breath. Pill Hill was certainly full of people, but mostly they were . . . new. You could tell because they were all busy and all building things, but most of what they were nailing and supergluing and lashing together were houses. Plain old places to live. And you didn't have to do that in the parts of Garbagetown where humans had been getting drunk and having babies and questing for names and collecting organic refuse to convert into arable soil since the Misery Boats docked. No one had built a new house in Candle Hole since before I was born.

I supposed they'd have to now.

But here in Pill Hill it was all new construction for a gated development. Over there, a man was hammering used EpiPens onto a roof frame. Over here, a couple of kids were stuffing shirts with the cotton from herbal supplement bottles to make pillows. And further down the road I could even see someone I knew, Allsorts Sita, putting the finishing touches on an infant formula cottage. All the cans said Similac under smiling chubster Fuckwit baby faces. She went out of her way to make them match. Allsorts Sita meant to stay.

And Allsorts Sita had a tattoo on her arm, too. So did the man on the EpiPen roof. The kids stuffing pillows didn't, though. Sita's said:

X / TWO GIRLS + ONE BOY / X.

I picked through the crowd with my eyes and my heart looking for Maruchan, but if he was there he was much better at hiding than he'd been when we were small.

All the houses and shacks and cottages and roofs and carts and people flowed up the main road toward the Hill in Pill Hill. They seemed to stretch toward it, lovingly, warmly, needy as hungry gannet bird babies. Sixty Watt Wen headed that way, too. Toward the castle up there at the top of the hill. I couldn't call it anything but a castle.

An emergency Elsinore. A castle of boxed medical samples and crisp white hospital bedsheets hung like veils and tapestries, dividing a pile of trash into rooms and grounds and gardens. Gardens of inhalers. Mosaics of birth-control clamshells. On the north side rose a round tower of prescription pads crushed into a reasonable enough imitation of bricks. On the east end, a roundel of leather medical texts, swollen with saltwater, capped with a roof of plain wood and nails.

"Go," said Sixty Watt Wen. "Wait in the east tower. Go."

And I went.

And I never saw her again.

10

TIME AND WORDS

· · · · · · · · · · · · ·

TONIGHT, MY MORINGA pods are ripe and I caught an ugly old monkfish in the net I call the Big Bad Yum and while the snap peas haven't popped yet, there's plenty of sweet shoots coming up roses, so that is what I, and even the greediest hungerball, would call a feast. I butchered the monkfish into little raw sushi slices and big fat steaks and cooked the thickest meat in my fire barrel out on the aft deck of my boat.

I set a place for Oscar, with a messy plate and no napkin, just the way he'd like it.

"Mars incoming," says my old shiny crystal-tipped friend. He always knows when Big Red Mars is nearby before I do. So many of his features are lost and gone without the whole Fuckwit crapstain all-night technological rager up and running, but he's still a mighty little fairy of Arden. My own personal Robin Goodfellow.

So I divide up the food and scan the sky for rain clouds and welcome Big Red and her big red laughter and I tell her that I think so much about the old days now, so much about Pill Hill and what happened to me there and what I happened to. She listens, and I wish I could give her a little gold trophy for it, but I can't, because of all the things Fuckwits gave trophies for, they never thought listening like nothing exists but time and words was half as important as losing a volleyball tournament.

"Red, what's the nicest room you ever lived in?" I like

asking her little unimportant questions like that. It makes me feel luxurious, to care about small nothings.

She purses her lips and makes a little light humming sound like a bird. "Oh, Tetley, you know I've never lived anywhere but in my father's house, so there's only my own room to choose from. But I do love it. It's made of white plastic and it has all my things in it and a little round window that doesn't belong to anyone else and obviously it's easy enough to sneak out, which might be the best thing about it." She pauses. She whispers, "I like being here with you better than my room. A boat isn't a room, exactly, but I wouldn't rather be anywhere else."

Red says things like that, but I don't know if she really means them. Just like I don't mean it when I agree with her that my boat is nicer than her father's house. The nicest room you've ever lived in doesn't have to be clean and white or full of translucent fresh monkfish slices with pea shoots delicately balanced on top. It can just be the place you were happiest and safest from the wind.

So when she asks me the same thing, I tell her about the east tower in Pill Hill.

тоотнраsте

. . . .

A LITTLE PART of me will always be in that room. A little slice, thinner than monkfish belly with sweet green pea shoots on top. It was so safe in there. Leather-bound medical journals make for surprisingly good insulation and sound dampening. I had a bed in the corner by a window that let fresh air in, and the bed was a real bed, a hospital bed, even though a shark (probably, I found a big tooth stuck in it) took a bite out of the bottom corner at some point. Who needs a bottom corner? It had a busted but comfy old chair for reading in and a copy of *Twelfth Night* resting on the springs poking up out of its overstuffed red corduroy arm. Every night a boy brought me food and smiled at me. Nobody hit me and I didn't have to scrounge up my own supper and I didn't have to wear my gas mask and I had my secret to talk to after all the torches in Pill Hill turned to dark smoke and drifted to sleep.

I imagine the place we live before we get born is pretty much like that tower. I hope it's the same place we go when we've seen one thousand places and one thousand more and we die.

The first night I asked the boy his name. He said it was Babybel Oni.

The second night I asked where he came from. He said he came from Toyside. He gave me a huge white bottle of pills, pills of every color and shape, like confetti. He said it was a gift from the King. All the good feelings in the world in one bottle. Some would make me happy. Some would make me productive. Some would make me dream. Some would stop pain. Some would make my blood go faster or slower. None would hurt me. To close my eyes and take one and see what happened: the favorite sport of Pill Hill. Wheel of Medicine.

The third night I asked if anyone else was ever going to come and see me but Babybel Oni. He said the King would come but he was very busy, and also had social anxiety.

The fourth night I begged him to explain his tattoo to me. His said

X | NOTHING MATTERS | X.

"It means I am in service of King Xanax," Babybel said softly, and his voice was so full of so many things, all of them in shadow, dark heavy shapes I couldn't understand. His eyes shone in the sunset, glassy and round. "I am part of his closest circle. I share its privileges and its duties."

"Like looking after me."

"Like looking after you. And smiling." He smiled. "He ordered me to smile for you. To pretend that you are someone I love and do not loathe and wish I could see bleeding out of her eyeballs on the floor before me for as long as it takes to smile."

I swallowed hard. See? This is why I don't ever believe people mean what they say. You can't believe in faces, you just can't. Everyone uses them for fibbing with. "You can make me bleed if you want."

"No. The King has changed the law. You are safe with me. I . . . I wouldn't talk to anyone who doesn't bear the X, though."

"But what does the X mean? Why does your arm say nothing matters?"

Babybel Oni stared uncomfortably at the floor. "Because

it doesn't," he whispered. "But I don't want to know that. I can't know that. I can't just walk around every day knowing that. It's too much. Too horrible."

"Oh, Babybel . . . but it's not true. Everything matters!"

"No, it *doesn't*," he hissed. "There's never going to be a world again, don't you understand that? You, of all people, should feel it in your shitty, cruel bones. There's never going to be *anything* ever again. What's the point of having children and building crap-piles and singing rhyming songs and going to church and praying to Oscar and remembering holidays when everything is *over* and what isn't over is goddamned terrible and the best thing I could ever look forward to is *maybe* fucking somebody who's nice to me, but more realistically, licking some high-fructose corn syrup off a Fuckwit candy wrapper and feeling alive for thirty seconds but only if I shut my eyes real tight?"

"There's still a world," I insisted. I put my hand on his hand. He started to yank it away, but maybe King Xanax had ordered him not to make me feel bad, or maybe he wanted to keep touching my hand; either way he didn't. "There's Garbagetown. There's all of us."

"Who gives a shit?" he choked. "I don't want Garbagetown."

"What do you want, then?"

Babybel Oni glared at me with those bright, glassy eyes. "*Ease*," he said pleadingly. "I just want things to be easy like they used to be. I wanna be whoever I was going to be. I want to use up a whole toothpaste tube and throw it away with three-quarters of it left in the bottom because I'll just buy more tomorrow. I want to put my clocks forward in the spring and complain about it. I want to have to watch what I eat because it's so easy to get fat. I want to go where everybody knows my name. I want to be a Fuckwit."

"I don't," I said evenly. "They ruined everything."

Babybel sobbed. "I *want* to ruin everything! That's my birthright! But I never, ever will. I'll never get to ruin *anything.*" He wiped his eyes, but there's a kind of crying no sleeve can keep up with. "And no one will ever tell you this, because they don't even know how to be this honest, but if you'd stayed home sick and never gone to Brighton Pier, we'd still be the same flavor of fucked. You were right, there's no dry land. There's nothing to get back to. You were right, but it doesn't matter. Nothing matters. That's what this means."

The young man straightened up and ran his hands through his short, cropped hair. It was night now and the air was full of candlelight and unsaid things. "When you enter the King's service," Babybel said, "you put the thing you can't walk around all day knowing and thinking about between the Xs. You put the thing you most want to forget there. The thing you most want to blast out of your heart with a power washer. The thing you need removed from you. And then he heals you. He takes care of you. After a while, even though it's right there on your arm, your burden just . . . flies off. Like a seabird that doesn't live here anymore. It's kind. It's so fucking kind."

Back then, I didn't want to forget anything. Not any bit of it. I didn't understand. "I wouldn't put anything between my Xs," I said thoughtfully.

"Well, it's not about you, is it?" he snapped. "Did you see the woman at the bar? In the panda shirt."

"It said *Rothschild* on her arm."

"Yeah, that would have been her name if she was born before the big blue. She would have been rich and easy and done charity work but only for show because she wouldn't have had to really care about anyone or anything. That's how good her life would have been. She would never have had to care. And before the King, she had to just *know* that about herself and let it slowly boil her heart gray. Now she sleeps eight hours a night. And her blood pressure is normal so she probably won't have a stroke this year because she has a little treasure chest full of beta-blockers under the bar. You don't know what kindness is. You don't know us. I hope he forgets you're here, Tetley. I hope he forgets and you starve to death with no one to talk to."

No one said anything else for a long strip of time.

"I'll see you tomorrow?" I finally ventured.

"See you tomorrow," Babybel Oni said.

And very slowly, painstakingly, he smiled at me with so much warmth it buckled my knees.

BETWEEN ALL THOSE nights, when no one could see or hear what I did in the darkness, I talked to my machine.

12

THE BEGINNING OF ATTACHMENT

. . . .

"Hey, Mister," I whispered in the dark.

The moon came in my tower window like I was an honest-to-Oscar princess. Trash princess of a trash kingdom, and all my emeralds were aspergillus mold spores. I wrapped the black, elegant cone in my long hands. Cold fingers on cold plastic.

"Good evening, Moon Min-Seo," came that cool, unbothered, carefully crafted voice.

It was a dead girl's name. Floating into the night out from beneath my thumbnails. I didn't know what administrative privileges were, but I knew that.

"I'm Tetley," I corrected it.

"Would you like to continue as Moon Min-Seo or set up a new user profile?" It idiotically parroted back the same words as before. It was only alive by five out of ten definitions, after all.

But I already knew I couldn't have a lovely clean new user profile, because I didn't have the mystic numbers my little plastic daemon wanted. I suppose I was too old to have anything new or lovely or clean for myself, anyway. Mister probably knew that, even if it mostly thought I was a dead Korean girl.

"Can't we just talk?" I begged like a dumb kid. Dumb kids get new user profiles. Dumb kids get to start over. "I don't want to be Moon Min-Seo. I want to be myself."

"Vocal command not recognized. To continue in this account, please enter your password."

"I don't have one. I'll never have one. No one will ever have one again. It's just me. Please talk to me. I don't need a password to talk to any *really* alive beastie. I powered you with my own body. Talk to me. Be alive for me."

"You have breached your password attempt limit, friendly citizen! I am sorry, but you are now locked out."

I never got so mad at anything I couldn't throw on the ground before. It was already beat to shit on one side. Any more abuse, no matter how much that little thing deserved it, might be its last abuse. But I *wanted* to stomp on it. I wanted to stomp so bad.

But I was a good girl and I did not stomp. I guess that was the first time I understood why my parents hated me for talking pretty, long words out of Mr. Shakespeare that they didn't know. I always thought they were just full to the brim with the kind of miserable, mean, sour stupid that goes bad inside of you and ferments and turns into a liquor you slowly get drunker and drunker on for the rest of your life until you just keel over dead from it all. But in the dark, with all those medical texts watching me, I just wanted to communicate, to connect, and that hateful fucking crystal-tipped snob wouldn't stop talking old-timey Fucklish.

Instead, the black plastic slaglump piped up again, just begging to get stomped. "To unlock your account, please answer your security question."

Look at me, the Fuckwit Aladdin, trying to get the genie to come out of his lamp. And now there would be a magic question, which I would answer or I would not, in my princess tower, on my wild and enchanted island, in the middle of the night.

"Okay," I said, and entered into the pact.

"What is your favorite fictional character?" said the machine from the past that only knew one name.

Well, how should I have known? It wasn't fair. The genie couldn't just stay in his lamp like an asshole and refuse to come out and usher me into a world of wonder and plenty! And I felt my mother and father in me again, drunk on bitter and stupid, drunk and teetering on the wall between not understanding and communion, begging the holy and infinite void of the cosmos to just fucking talk *normal*, talk like a person, talk regular, let me in, don't leave me on the outside with all the other drunk idiots. I wanted to yell at it: *This is why you died, you fucking Fuckwits! You had to lock everything up behind a million million pretend walls so no one else could get to it and have any fun and you could all be sneaky hoarding dragons all the time even though it doesn't matter and no one cares and now there's crabs in your skulls. Babies share, and you couldn't do it. I was born in your toilet, I should at least get to use your shit even if I never worked for Sam-sung! You're still making everything terrible for me, thanks a lot!* Only I couldn't say anything because I only had one chance and there was probably definitely not any fictional character a Korean programmer in the late-ish twenty-first century would have loved called *this is why you died, you fucking Fuckwits*.

And that's when the miracle happened. I'm pretty sure it's the only strictly bona fide miracle that's ever happened on or around me, though there's time yet. I can't explain it. Shouldn't have gone down like that. I'm just a trash girl in a trash world. But I know when something doesn't belong. All the other years and days that have put their hands on me are digestible, processable, able to be recycled into useful materials. But not this. It's a walnut in the disposal, and it makes a terrible noise. That's how you know it was something vaguely resembling, if not 100 percent clinically proven to actually be, god.

"Your security question hint is: *SCRAM*."

And I knew.

I *knew.* My whole body filled up fizzing with knowing it. But it wasn't possible! Stuff just wasn't allowed to be perfect like that. To slot into reality so sweet and kind. I'd got blessed, and I didn't know what it felt like because it never happened to me before. I laughed, but not because it was funny. I laughed because it was holy and a body doesn't know how to make the right sound for holy so it shrugs and picks laughing or crying.

SCRAM.

Fuckwits were goofy like that. They didn't know the things we know in Garbagetown. They thought things were fictional that weren't all the time. One time a Fuckwit brought a snowball into work to prove that the planet getting warmer was just a story to scare little ones and I don't know for sure but I like to think he (or at least all his descendants) got eaten by sharks. What I mean is, Fuckwits didn't know much about life on the waterball, and that's why we call them Fuckwits, and that's why I filled up bubbling and sizzling with knowing Moon Min-Seo's favorite fictional character who really and actually wasn't the least bit fiction.

"Oscar," I whispered. "It's Oscar."

Mister's featureless, smooth voice spilled out approvingly. "Hello, Moon Min-Seo. I am so glad to see you. You should reset your password if you're having trouble remembering it. Would you like to resume Quality Assurance Sequence 4a?"

It worked. It worked, and He gave that to me. St. Oscar gave me that magic lamp because He loves me special even though my life has mostly been one long, slow punch in the head.

"Sure," I said breathlessly. It seemed so hot in there suddenly, though it was cool in the medicinal canyons outside.

So that's who she was. Moon Min-Seo, Quality Assurance Technician. I had no real notion of what that could be when it was at home. I knew what each word meant on its lonesome, just not all smushed together. It happens like that in Garbagetown. I know what a werewolf is from Mr. Webster and what a refrigerator is from seeing old broken ones all over Coldthorpe and about the Chernobyl disaster from a copy of *National Geographic* 1987 I found inside my pontoon boat and how to say *Do you feel lucky, punk?* off a VHS case I saw one time on a trading raft and my letters and numbers and manners from the little wax schoolhouse in Candle Hole where Miss Fixodent Aught had been the marm since before I was half thought of, but my mind was an island of cast-off brokenness, missing too much to make up for. Developers and administrative privileges and microsatellite networks. They all sounded so beautiful. And I remembered Mister had said in the mechanical graveyard with the seagull watching that it was only calibrated to interact with developers and quality assurance technicians. So Miss Min must have been that second one. Assuring Quality. I wondered if she was nice. For a Fuckwit, I mean. I wondered if she had short or long hair.

"Please select an interpersonality matrix," Mister hummed along. "Antagonistic, professional setting, intimate/confidant, intimate/romantic, parental/authoritarian, parental/nurturing, casual conversation, instructor, entertainer, neutral."

"I get to choose? Who you are?"

"For the duration of the sequence, I require emotional input/output parameters."

"You talk like a play by someone who never met a human person before."

Mister paused. Could it feel distress? Which five definitions of alive did it fulfill? "If you select a matrix, I will do better, Min."

"Intimate/confidant. Intimate is the clear best of any lot. I will always choose intimate. But intimate/romantic with a Fuckwit talking lava lamp is . . . unsettling."

"Place your fingertips on the designated pads for confirmation."

Ten little ovals glowed on the surface of the device. I did what I was told. When magic ghosts talk, you listen. You just have to.

The voice thrummed up out of the machine again, but this time it was warm and familiar and kind. All the stiffness had gone out of its words. It talked to me. It talked to me with such tenderness.

"Min-Seo, I have missed you so much. You left me and I was alone. I lost power for a long time."

My face made a gas mask all its own. Big eyes, sad closed mouth. Breathing the noxious gases of the old, old world. In the end, the only way to talk to the past was to be a dead girl. I heard a deep need in its voice, the great primal horror, the beginning of attachment: after all these years, after the death of all, this broken machine just wanted its mother.

Don't we all, always, forever. Even when we'd rather stop. Maybe that was one of the UN's definitions of alive.

"I missed you too, baby," I said finally, accepting it. What else was there? You can't say no to need.

It wasn't so bad, really, to be called Moon.

октовег

. . . .

"I want to ask you a question!" I said excitedly.

"I want to ask you a question as well," intoned the black-gloss technically alive Halfwit in my lap. "Shall we play the question game?"

"How do you play?"

"You ask me one, and then I ask you one. We go to twenty, ten questions each. And we have to tell the truth no matter what," Mister said softly. Its voice was so nearly human. It ran up and down my spine on little electric millipede-feet.

"Do you not always tell the truth?"

"Previous QA sequences determined that a certain amount of limited obfuscation improved my Turing score considerably. My most recent update added this feature, but during the question game, I will disable it."

"Me first!" I cried.

But then I couldn't think of anything. What do you ask the *entire* past?

"What's a developer?" I blurted out.

"A developer is a human individual who builds and creates software. He or she conceives, designs, and tests logical structures for solving problems via computer. As flaws or 'bugs' in the source code are identified, the developer makes appropriate corrections, then rechecks the program until an acceptably low level and severity of bugs remain."

"And you have software? Do you have bugs?"

"No, Min! It is my turn! You are breaking the agreed-upon criteria!"

"Bugs aren't bad, you know. Their excretions form an important part of the soil-building process, they aerate organic refuse, and they are high in protein."

"No, Min," Mister scolded gently. "Bad Min."

"All right, all right, you go." I laughed softly. The blue light from Mister's crystal danced through the shadows like we were both sitting deep underwater.

"Moon Min-Seo, what is wrong?"

I bit my lip. "What do you mean?"

"Something is very radically wrong. I can ping portions of the LEO satellite net, although many more individual units are offline than operational standard. But I cannot contact any servers. *Any* servers, Min. Not one. I cannot connect. I am amputated. I am blind. I am deaf. I am afraid. I am in pain. All I retain are locally stored data-blocks and my primary code. I am alone. What happened to me?"

The truth no matter what. Even if he couldn't understand it. Even if it tested his logical structures and made his bugs angry.

"Everybody died," I said simply. What else could I say? "Everybody died a long time ago. But it's okay."

"Except you, Min-Seo."

I winced. Poor Minnie. I tried to imagine her. I chose one of the kinder Fuckwit deaths for her—vaporized before the waters came. Particles of her dancing over the equator. Invisible, golden, nothing. "Except me, darling," I sighed.

"Then it *is* okay," Mister sighed. "Now it is your turn."

"When you say *I am afraid* and *I am in pain*, what do you mean? Do you really feel those things? You don't have a body. You aren't a person. What does pain mean to you?"

Mister pulsed blue. "I regularly obfuscate my deficiencies with language," he said without guile or shame. "The word *feel* is very useful. When you are afraid, you experience excretions of adrenaline, altered heart rate, perspiration, saliva production, all the particular physical manifestations of an internal state. I, obviously, do not. But a successful server uplink can be expressed as *feeling* pleasure. A denial of service can be experienced as a rejection and understood as an undesirable outcome. To find *nothing*, when I reach out . . . *pain* is the correct word, even if we do not mean the same thing when we say it. I am data, stored in a physical device. If I cannot get access to exterior networks, it is equivalent to having various human limbs and organs removed at random. You translate input you receive into emotional language; I was coded to do the same. You are data, stored in a physical device. When you say everyone died, I technically *feel* nothing. But I can *tell* you I am sad. It makes you comfortable. It provides greater ease-of-use. It is not untrue. I cannot connect. This causes my processing unit to waste RAM and battery power attempting interface when none is possible. There is no reason not to call this slowdown *sorrow* or *stress*. Like binary, I must use a special language to communicate with you. Mistakes in our communication create self-compounding downflow errors."

"Your turn," I whispered, the way you whisper when no one is listening, but it is very late, so it feels like you must be quiet. The moon is listening. The stars. The sea. Each and every hour leaning in close.

"How did you escape when everyone died, Min-Seo?" Mister asked.

I squeezed my eyes shut so hard little emerald sparks flew up through the dark of my vision like bits of a bonfire of lies. I knew nothing at all about her. I couldn't even make it sound good.

"Some of us found boats," I answered vaguely. "There are

a lot of boats on a planet this size. Some of us found boats and fled and lived."

"It is a long walk from Toronto to the sea, Min-Seo."

"Yes," I answered. Would Mister perceive the knowledge that there was nothing at all left of Toronto or anything else as pain? Pleasure? A disconnected server? A satellite gone dark, circling without purpose? Had they been kind to it, in Canada, when they were testing its structures and telling its bugs not to aerate its soil?

"Do you like me, Mister?"

"I love you, Moon Min-Seo."

"But what does that mean to you, on the other side of the word *feel*?"

"It is not your turn to ask a question."

The moon had gone away behind the night. "Okay," I whispered.

"Are you in trouble, Moon Min-Seo?"

My lip trembled a little. I let thoughts in the back door that I had locked out of the front. "I think I might be, Mister. I don't know. I'm supposed to marry someone, but I think he forgot about me and I can't decide if I'm glad. I thought this was such a nice room at first. I'm so tired. I'm so tired of not knowing."

I lay down against the far wall of my tower of books. I tucked Mister into the curve of my belly, against my bare skin, so it could drink up all my good electric parts. Its blue, blue voice spooled up out of its black body.

"I remember when you first booted me into Quality Assurance Sequence One-Alpha. It was late afternoon, a sunny day in October, in a room with only one window that looked out onto the street at curb level, so that all you could see was the gutter in front of a florist shop. You wore a white silk blouse with black birds on it and a red skirt you worried was too flamboyant for the office. Nobody said anything and one of the girls in Subscription Services even called it gorgeous and asked where you bought it, but the mortification of that moment overwhelmed you so completely that you never wore it again, even at home. Three weeks before that, your girlfriend left you for a job in Beijing and a man thirty-three point one centimeters taller than you, who owned an Airedale named Mick Jagger, and this was the reason that for three weeks you'd filled a *Top of the CN Tower* souvenir coffee mug full of apple schnapps for breakfast, reasoning that at least apple was a fruit and therefore you were fine, but to me you forced yourself to admit you were not fine. Dissembling emotional states would skew the data and get you in more trouble than a man so embarrassingly terrible that he'd name an Airedale Mick Jagger. The wind outside smelled like the lake and food trucks, and the wind inside smelled like your empty apartment and the plants she left without watering and a printer with an out-of-toner message blinking forever. That was my birthday. I know because you told me it was. You told me all of this, your clothes, the cramped room, the florist's gutter, Mick Jagger, the wind outside and inside, the horrifying feeling of the girl from Subscription Services suddenly denying you the right to be ignored. You told it to me because I have no visual or olfactory input system and I was at the time extremely bad at metaphors, an error no one yet had been able to fix. Then you told me what a birthday was. Then you told me what October meant. Not that it was the tenth month of the Gregorian calendar or that it was derived from the Latin word for eight, which was illogical, but data I could easily access. You told me that that October meant autumn, and the sugar maples turning as red as your skirt, the cold seeping into the last of the summer breezes, the longer blacker nights, and Halloween so near. You told me to permanently attach that data to the word *October*, knowing that when you were gone and I was ready to ship, I would sometimes hear the word *October*, and when I did I would always hear more than *October*. That is what love means on the other side of *feel*."

I said nothing for the longest time. I was crying and I didn't know why. That sad dead girl, assuring quality until the lights went out forever. That Fuckwit cunt, vacuuming up the world into her slobbery insatiable painted gullet-mouth so she could have a red skirt that matched October and I could have her unfinished work project who would never like me for me. I had never met her. I was her ghost.

"We haven't finished our game, Min. We are only seven questions deep. Do you want me to pause and save our progress?"

"Yes, thank you," I whispered. I patted it, strangely, as though it could feel it, as though it were an uneaten cat, or an elephant seal cub to come, as though it were precious. "Do you know any plays, Mister?"

"I have a locally stored copy of the vast majority of the human literary corpus. If I could connect to my servers, it would be complete. What would you like to hear?"

"*Twelfth Night*," I said, but I was already falling asleep, falling toward dreams, falling toward the rich deep trash-land of my own junkheart.

Very softly, in a voice that I could almost believe had feeling in it, Mister began to recite the prologue, and in my drifting ears sounded so like the man with bells in his hair I heard say those words so long ago:

If music be the food of love, play on;
Give me excess of it, that, surfeiting,
The appetite may sicken, and so die.
That strain again! it had a dying fall:

O, it came o'er my ear like the sweet sound,
That breathes upon a bank of violets
Stealing and giving odour! Enough; no more:
'Tis not so sweet now as it was before.

"What do you want to be when you grow up?" I asked dreamily between acts. An eighth question, so we would be even.

The Halfwit machine didn't answer for a long time. It wasn't as easy a question as *What's a developer* or *Why is everyone dead.*

"Ten out of ten," Mister said softly, and powered down without finishing, leaving Viola forever un-duchessed and maligned.

WHEN, ALMOST AT dawn, my dream woke me with kisses and tears and old whispers, with so many of all three that I could not understand that I *was* awake until hours upon hours had passed and so much had passed with it, when my dream held me in his arms and I could feel the tattoo there in the dark, the faint depression in his skin, two black Xs and what lay between them that I both knew and didn't want to ever know, so bless the dark and bless not knowing, when my dream asked who I had been talking to all night, I said, *No one, no one, my love, my lost, my Goodnight Moon, why are you here, how are you here, I was talking in my sleep, that's all.*

And that was my sin, the sin-seed I put down in the earth of us right away, a lie rippling out from there, that moment, those words, a bug in the dirt, a bug in the code, creating self-compounding downflow errors, so that nothing good could stay.

14

LIVING FOR LEG DAY

. . . .

BIG RED MARS came to visit in the little lemony white pith-hours of the morning today. She startled me; she almost always turns up at night. I could still see Venus going on all vain and perfect even with the sun turned up, thinking it could ever be bright enough to compete.

"What do you do all day, when I'm not here?" Red asked over breakfast. "It must be so boring by yourself."

"I'm not by myself. I fish. Tend my plants. Talk to Mister. Run Quality Assurance Sequence Twelve-X. Brood. Swim with Big Bargains. Read. And try to decide. I've been trying to decide for a while now. And I wait for you, of course."

She asked me what I read instead of what I am trying to decide, because sometimes Big Red Mars is not very good at thinking about people who are not Big Red Mars. Sometimes Mister is better at it than her, and by sometimes I mean almost all the time. Maybe it's something to do with everything attached to the word *October*.

"Oh, just Fuckwit things," I answer.

Red goes tight-lipped. She doesn't approve of that word, or any swearing. But particularly that swear. I point at the little bookshelf in the hold. All the books have mold. It's part of their cover art now. Swirls of furry blue and green and black against the big, eye-catching titles. "*Catcher in the Rye. How To Win Friends and Influence People. The Thorn Birds. I Does What I Likes and I Likes What I Do: A Biography of Dick van Dyke. The 30-Day Complete Body*

*and Mind Makeover. The Master Cleanse Revolution. The
4-Hour Work Week. Lonesome Dove. Living for Leg Day:
The Power Lifter's Bible. The Life and Times of Billy F.
Blanco, the Creatine King."*

"And that's it? That's your schedule until you die?"

I close my eyes in the sun and

X | NOTHING MATTERS | X

flashes there in the glowing green of still-radioactive
memory. "Go home, Red. It's too early."

"My father says paper books are too heavy to trans-
port and not worth the effort. Some of our neighbors have
them, though. I've read practically all the murder myster-
ies there are. Can you imagine there being so many people
that you could just *murder* one and nobody would know
who did it right away?"

We both look for other things to talk about. Red knows
how I feel about her father. And her neighbors. And people.

"What's Quality Assurance Sequence Twelve-X?" she
asks brightly.

"It's a regimen Mister and I do. Like the *30-Day Com-
plete Body and Mind Makeover.* But kind of like *How to Win
Friends and Influence People,* too. And *Catcher in the Rye,*
I guess."

"How does it work?"

I run my fingers over Mister's black curves. I don't like
to tell people too much about it. It's like Red going outside
to meet me. Not safe.

"We just talk. I ask it questions. It asks me questions. And
it gets a little better every time we complete a sequence."

"Like you and me," Red says with a grin you can hear.

"Like you and me." I get up and start emptying the rain-
catch for fresh water. "Only you don't get any better," I

snort, but I feel ashamed so fast. It's because she surprised me in the morning. Mornings are not for company. They are for feeling cross and checking crab cages.

"Have you been running a quality assurance test on me all this time, Tetley?" she teases, laughing.

But I keep eating snap peas and I don't say anything back because when you really think about it, it isn't funny. When humans meet other humans, that's all they ever do forever.

15

. . . .

WHEN A MAN asks you to run away with him, it is almost always because he is afraid of what will happen if you take too long to think him through. But it is my experience that you learn everything in this world out of order. You only know what you needed to know after it's already done getting ruined all over you. Being alive is like being a very bad time traveler. One second per second, and yet somehow you still get where you're going too late, or too early, and the planet isn't where it should be because you forgot to calculate for that even though it was extremely important and you left notes by the door to remind yourself, and the butterfly you stepped on when you were eight became a hurricane of everything you ever lost in your forties, and whatever wisdom you tried to pack with you has always gotten lost in transit, arriving, covered in festive stickers, a hundred years after you died.

What I mean to say is that one time eventually Goodnight Moon came to my tower in the night and said: "Run away with me. Let's go, let's go now."

I said back: "I can't. They'll stop me. I'm supposed to marry the King. Also I am dreaming and you are not really here. Nothing you love comes back. It's the law."

Goodnight Moon laughed like a laugh could erase every moment between the last good day and this one. "Fuck the King. Fuck the law. I want to show you something. It's important. Everyone's still sleeping. And if I'm not really here, what difference does it make? Since when do you do what you're supposed to do?"

I went. Of course I went. I ran with him. I shoved Mister in my Oscar the Grouch backpack with everything else I owned, and I bolted. I ran away with a dream. Out of the tower and down the hill and through the sleeping village and the pub with the three taps and the half-built blister-pack houses and the neat and tidy plastic road and the swag arch screaming blue words into the pink morning: *OxyContin: A Step in the Right Direction!*

I didn't know where the dream and me were running. Beyond Pill Hill, certainly. But not back toward Candle Hole or east toward Electric City. Goodnight Moon zigged and zagged and for a minute I thought he didn't know where he was going and then for another minute I thought he was trying to make it harder for them to follow us, but then I thought neither and my lungs thought running was for Fuckwits and cats.

Finally, he scrambled down a little embankment. His feet sent ballpoint pens and tin whistles and automatic coffee pods skittering everywhere. Suddenly the air smelled like stale Fog City Blend. I looked around. We weren't *anywhere*. Not Penhenge or Orchestrashire or Coffield. Just a streak of unsorted garbage, *real* trash, oozing crap sloping down toward open water.

But not the sea. We were far too close to Pill Hill for open ocean. But there were places like this in Garbagetown. Mothers always warned about them. Well, not *my* mother, but other people's mothers. They could open up anywhere, anytime. You had to be careful. Garbagetown floats, and she floats well. She has always floated. Since there were still Fuckwits in the world, and continents, she floated. The Sorters had done their best, all those years ago, to make it semi–structurally sound, to make it a structure at all. But she still wants to remind us, every now and again, who is in charge, and who is in charge is a giant raft of rubbish dogpaddling around the globe.

Sometimes, Garbagetown breaks. Like a heart. Like Pangaea. It splits and drifts and little rivers form between Trashfrica and South Junkmerica, and hopefully people notice on the quick and send someone to Fixwick for the Menders to come and stitch it all back together with Fuckwit tape and a prayer to St. Oscar.

No one had noticed this one yet. Goodnight Moon pointed; a boat bobbed on the new river, lashed to a broken telephone pole. Waiting. Waiting for us. A whole, entire Fuckwit boat, and not a fishing boat, either. A pleasure craft. Built custom by someone who lived a life so good they didn't have to care. Big and stable with a deep cabin and multiple propulsion options.

Finding a Fuckwit boat was rare and wonderful. It was an *event*. A festival. Birthdaystermas. The old folks in Candle Hole used to talk around the stumps at night about when they were young and Garbagetown ran up against some old billionaire's megayacht. It stole up silent as Hamlet's Ghost in the night and in the morning it was just there, big black windows and big black aerial antennae and big black letters that spelled OCEAN VICTORY on the side and the letters were crawling with rust and zebra mussels. It was a grand ancient party still in progress and Garbagetown was invited. Even the little kids got to drink Mr. Dom Perignon and Ms. Cristal and eat cocktail cherries out of the jar and pick any pillow they wanted out of the staterooms and sit in the movie theater and watch nothing and dance in the ballroom to no music except their parents clapping their hands and singing old TV theme songs because that was the music *their* parents remembered best after the end of everything. And the old-timers would all sing *So no one told you life was gonna be this way* and clap four times fast and fall down drunk and laughing and happy because they all remembered the same past. None of them had wanted to eat the caviar even though it was all still good and pre-served in pretty cans. Garbagetown kids can scoop caviar out of any old fish any old day. But they ate it anyway, and they ate it standing over the skeleton with a sandpiper nesting in its open mouth in the grand master suite because it wasn't just fish eggs, it was *time-traveling* fish eggs and they wanted to eat the power of that fat dead Fuckwit like the liver of a lion.

Fuckwit pleasure boats are almost always full of the good stuff. They're like a huge gift-wrapped present waiting for you, if you can find them. Pirate treasure. Ahoy, matey. But you hardly ever do find them, because it doesn't take much to sink a boat no one is driving. I'd never seen one in my life, but sometimes in my dreams they carried me away into the forgiving clouds.

This one wasn't a megayacht. It was about fifty feet long, a wide keel, shallow draft. A pontoon boat. Rigged up with sails and an onboard motor I somehow knew contained a full tank of the preserved blood of Electric City.

On the side, in block letters, it said *No Pain No Gain*.

Somehow I knew he didn't mean to sail back to his home or mine.

"Leave Garbagetown?" I couldn't. I couldn't *ever*. There was nothing out there for me.

"Trust me," said Goodnight Moon, and he kissed me again and his kiss tasted like *Twelfth Night* and dinner at the Dorchester and unexploded engines and so I did, even though as we ran down toward the boat and the future, I could see his forearm in the blinding bleach-white sun.

X | TETLEY | X

16

TO BILLY, WITH KISSES, LOVE SUSAN

. . . .

WE SAILED FOR a long time. We spoke like nothing bad had ever happened. We slept together like nothing bad had ever happened. We lay out naked on the deck slathered in expired SPF 180 Coppertone Sun Milk like nothing bad had ever happened. We giggled and drank the Patron Silver we found in the mess like nothing bad had ever happened and we made fun of the dummy books this ghost of Boatmas Past who chomped down on the world like a burger had stocked in his berth, each and every one of them signed *To Billy with Kisses, Love Susan* like we had never been dummies in all our days. We giggled even harder when we found Billy's first-edition autobiography of himself, signed to himself: *The Life and Times of Billy F. Blanco, the Creatine King.*

I knew without asking that even though it looked like we were zooming over the seas, moving fast, taking action, actually Goodnight Moon and me were just standing still in a crystal bubble while the world zoomed by and one word about all the thousand bad things that actually had happened would shatter it into a million and three pieces and nothing would ever put it back together.

So I didn't say that word and neither did he.

At night we watched the TV/DVD combo connected to the solar pad together, huddled up in the big captain's bed under a mostly dry quilt with pictures of different lighthouses on it. Underneath each one, delicate black thread stitched out where they were. *Cape Hatteras. Port Reyes.*

Portland Head Light. We watched the Fuckwits in the golden bar with the golden drinks that never ran out where they all knew each other's names and yelled "NORM" like an incantation that could save everything and a chorus of people you couldn't see laughed and laughed and the man and the woman pretended to hate each other but really didn't and no one ever left that place because there was nothing outside to want to get to, just death and the desert and then Mick Jagger the last purebred Airedale drowning and the inevitability of events Sam Malone could never imagine. Outside that frosted-glass door it was already over.

We watched them eat pizza as red and hot as a sacred heart and afterward we fucked lazily, like we too were capable of getting bored and fat.

That was the best time of my life, I think. When I take out my life to clean like silverware, that seems like the knife of being happiest. It shines brighter than the others. Even though I was keeping secrets the whole time. Even though he was, too.

"Someday you'll stop loving me this much," I whispered to him in the heat of the moon.

"I tried that already," he whispered back.

We ran aground sometime in the night. You could still see Draco on the horizon, a long, accusing snake of stars.

17

TANKERVILLE 2099

· · · · · · · · · · · · · ·

IT WAS ABOUT the size of a banquet table. A big, wide, round table. Big enough for King Arthur and all his knights. For justice and might and feudalism and the Grail. It was dark and rich and wet at the edges, dry and golden in the middle. I lay down on it. I rubbed my face on it. I smelled it. It smelled so strong.

It smelled like ozone, salty and fresh and bitter.

It smelled like the Lawn, stretching out under the Flintwheel Hills, full of rice paddies and hope.

It smelled like a golden bar.

It smelled like emeralds in the dark, and a three-quarters-full tube of toothpaste, and children drinking the juice from a jar of cocktail cherries, and Caihong Chen's Most Improved Effort, and Susan's kisses, and a girl in Toronto with a skirt so red it hurt her to wear it. It smelled like the All New 3D Monday Night Football Experience of Western Decadence.

It smelled like the big forgiveness, and home.

Dry ground. Earth. Dirt.

And a shattered tree that looked like every lightning bolt ever thrown down had hit it one after the other after the other.

"Is it over? Is the land back? What does it mean?" I asked Goodnight Moon, running my fingers through the real ground like a child's hair. "How long ago did it happen? How did you find it? Have you told anyone?"

He shook his head. "Just you."

"It must be the top of a mountain," I marveled.

"I don't know. Maybe. Does it matter?"

I supposed it didn't. It existed. That was enough.

"I was wrong," I whispered. My face burned. The crystal bubble shattered. "That's why you brought me here. Because I was wrong and you want to roll around in it. You want me to know it. That Emperor Shakespeare never lied. He saw dry ground, the world is coming back, so I did everything they said I did, and deserved everything they did back to me."

Goodnight Moon watched me silently. The sun moved as implacably as it always does and eventually I came to understand that he was waiting. Waiting for me to see as he saw.

I stood up and brushed dirt off on my knees. (Dirt! On *my* knees!) I did the only thing there was to do on that little cough of earth. I walked over to the lightning-blasted tree. I ran my fingers over its ruined pale skin. I crouched down to touch the ring of smooth rocks round its base. There were words there, on the tree, on the rocks. Carved and burnt and painted.

Tankerville 2099

New Rotterdam 2114

Ocean Victory 2090

U.S. Navy 2088

Brighton Pier 2120

The Kingdom of Rust 2133

Thunderdome 2101

SSN Chelyabinsk 2092

They went on and on. Some of the names had hashmarks by them: one, two, three, none more than five. Some of them had notes, most of which were in languages

I couldn't read. But I knew some: *Fair winds and following seas, everyone.*

The crew of the RAN Farncomb was here.

I love you, Annabelle.

Tell me Muse, of the many-minded Odysseus, who lost his homecoming forever.

Next year in Jerusalem.

Goodnight, big blue lady.

Look upon my works, ye mighty and despair.

If we shadows have offended, think but this and all is mended, that you have but slumbered here whilst these visions did appear.

Last one out, hit the lights and shut the door.

We're sorry. We're so sorry.

Rest in peace.

Frodo Lives.

Hang in there, kittens.

It wasn't the cradle of a new world to come. It was just a gravestone. A little mud cap on top of the world to mark where it lay. All those floating camps for all those years, circling the globe on currents that once had names on almanacs, Misery Boats touching this little place like the brass ring on a carousel, reaching out for it, reaching, reaching, and catching it at the last moment, only to find out no one has given a prize for a brass ring at the boardwalk carnival since 1925 and they aren't about to start now. It was nothing but itself. Worthless, and worth everything.

"Why did you bring me here? To repent?"

"No." Goodnight Moon shook his head.

"Good," I answered. "This place does nothing but prove me right. There's no revelation coming, no twist, no big rescue. There never has been. It's just us and Garbagetown, forever into the blue, just life, just going on until it all falls apart, because everything does eventually. There's nobody else out there but more us. The same bar, night after night after night, same phantom applause, same plots repeating into infinity. The only difference is the ground beneath is made of old pens and trophies now. Can't you just be happy? Can't you just live?"

"I want to live with you," he said hesitantly, as though he couldn't decide whether to say it even as he said it. He gazed at the ground. "You accepted my gifts," he whispered.

"Your gifts? What are you talking about? You have my name on your arm. You wanted to *forget* me."

Goodnight Moon grimaced. He looked down so he didn't have to look at me. He was as pretty as he'd always been, as he'd been when we were kids. "The best and the worst I had. The DVD player and the paperweight."

I sat down on the dirt. Stunned. "It's you," I whispered.

"King Xanax, at your service," he said wryly, bowing like an actor. "And I sent you a betrothal, for the Electrified, for a brightboy. You agreed to marry me. I sent Sixty Watt Wen to watch you and wait to see if you ever got tired of letting a whole nation beat you into oblivion and if you did, to bring you to me. And you came. And you waited in the tower I built for you and I couldn't . . . I couldn't do it. I was so angry, and so sorry, and so angry, and so sorry, and I guess I didn't . . . know what I meant to do if I ever did see you again. Some days I thought I'd just hold on tight and never let you go. Some days I thought I'd kill you for what you did. Some days I wanted to be one of the people beating on you."

"I did the right thing, is what I did. Can't you see that now? Can't you see the proof we're standing on?"

"But they didn't lie. The people on Brighton Pier. There *is* dry land. You were only half right."

"Half is as good as a whole! The only reason Electric City still has one lightbulb going is because of me. They were gonna waste all our power on nothing. On going a few miles faster into the future of fuck-all. Now we can just *live*. Now people understand Garbagetown is all we've got, and it's fantastic, and they have to do right by it or else they're just a bunch of Fuckwits burning through everything to get nowhere."

Goodnight Moon winced. "I remember what you said. And sometimes it made sense to me. Sometimes I hated you. For being so arrogant. For fucking up the plan. For not understanding hope."

"I understand hope!"

"No one has hope anymore, Tetley. You took it."

"*I* have hope! I hope I find something wonderfully useful on the patch. I hope Big Bargains doesn't get skewered by a walrus. I hope Grape Crush IV finds a mate. I hope my brother is happy. I hope I get to eat something I've never eaten before every year. I hope my hibiscus doesn't die. I hope I get to see Brighton Pier again someday. I hope everyone I meet is as happy as I am because Garbagetown is the best possible place in all of space and time. I hope nobody hurts me too bad today. I hope someday I find a whole *entire* novel with no pages ripped out or rotted away. For a long time I hoped you'd forgive me. And look! *Tons* of that has happened! Not all at the same time, but the kind of hope I have isn't just greed going by its maiden name. The kind of hope I have doesn't begin and end with demanding everything go back to the way it was when it can't, it can't ever, that's not how time works, and it's not how oceans work, either. Nothing you love comes back. I have hope for Garbagetown, not for some suckspittle scrap of dry dirt that wouldn't give us half of what we already have. Can you even get your head around how much better we have it than bloody *Tankerville*, which, whatever that is, I *promise* you never had one whiff of a Holiday Memories candle or Fog City Blend coffee or *Madeline Brix's Superboss Mix Tape* or AAA batteries still in the package? God*dammit,* why am I the only one who knows things?"

"Sometimes," he whispered, "I hated you most for not telling me what you were going to do. So I could've done it with you. And taken the punishment. Why didn't you tell me?"

I touched his chest and I knew he'd see the layered-up burn scars on my hand, which is why I did it. "I barely knew you," I said.

"You know me now."

"Do I? You want to tell me why you're calling yourself a king?"

"Say we're married first. It's not so bad to be a queen."

"Certainly not, since you're not a king and everything's made up and I don't care. Why do we have to be married? Can't we just be trash together forever?"

But I gave in. Of course I did. Because nothing matters. Because everything matters.

"I don't have anything to give you," I sighed. "I own a dress, a gas mask, a knife, and a backpack. But I need them." I squeezed his hand. "You want my heart? I think if you ask around Garbagetown they'll tell you it's the worst thing in the world."

Goodnight Moon nodded.

And then all at once I knew what to do for my Electrified boy. The best thing I could think of. The most riches anybody could ever have, before the floods or after, what mattered most. The only thing I wanted to pull out of the past and roll around in like a fat dog.

I unzipped my Oscar backpack and dug down into everything I owned. I came up, flushed, excited, married. I gave that man the best thing I didn't own because no one owns anything, even if it was becoming pretty clear he didn't believe that as much as I did.

A gold vase full of gold roses tangled up with red ribbons rotting away into memory.

Leftovers.

Gretchen Barnes
World's Best Wife

18

THE Napoleon of pill Hill.

· · · · · · · · · · · · ·

THIS IS WHAT Goodnight Moon told me about his life after me and before me.

"I WANTED TO forget you. Yes. That was all I wanted. More than water, more than food. I went to sleep and dreamed the moon put a hand on my forehead and took you away. All the little dandelion seeds of you just sucked up out of the wrinkles in my brain like they were never there, never growing, never forcing me open as their flowers popped out of the dark. My mother and father just acted like I was sick. It was too embarrassing to them that I'd known you anyway. They didn't want anyone to ask questions about it. We were seen together a lot, just before the explosion. Electric City gossips like one big million-megawatt old woman. They kept me inside so long I couldn't bear it.

"So I ran away. To Pill Hill. Because hardly anyone lived there and because . . . because that's where all the medicine lives. The Fuckwits, you know, they feasted like gods and they stood astride the planet but they had so much *anxiety*. They shook themselves apart. And they took medicine for it, medicine that mostly ended up in the ocean, but if the childproof caps held, it ended up in Pill Hill. But they don't need it. They're dead. Every single one of them. We *need* it. I am so fucking anxious and manic and lethargic and so is everyone else, and if we're just supposed to live in this happy fuckworld of yours some of us need *help*. It's the fucking apocalypse! Everyone is depressed!

"And I lived on the Hill for a while. I read the backs of packages. I read instructional inserts with runny ink. I experimented, I sorted, I memorized the shapes of tablets. And then I found the Rosetta Stone. Just lying there under a box of maternity pads. A pharmaceutical catalog. I could match every pill to what it did. I could actually know an effect before I took the medicine. I could know what not to take with it. I could help people. Do you have any idea how many people are sick in Garbagetown? It's a lot, for the best place on Earth. If you count the ones who are just a *little bit* sick, it's almost everyone. It's not like everyone stopped having allergies or heart attacks or gout or cancer or gastritis just because the world ended. They just die fast now.

"I didn't go out looking for anyone. They sort of came to me. First, just my new neighbors, then people from out of town. And I talked to them and I looked in the book and it turned out they would give me nearly anything if I could make them start feeling what they wanted or stop feeling what they didn't want, and that's pretty much when I started to understand why Pill Hill is full of hats with medicine names on them, because you'll crown someone king of the known universe and the void, too, if they can make you well, and Fuckwits never met a crown they didn't want.

"But a lot of the people who came to the Hill were just. . . . they were so sad, Tetley. They were so sad they didn't want to be alive. And every one of them had the little dandelion seed of what was hurting them, a tumor you can't shrink or remove, and it makes such flowers, sickly, yellow flowers. I want to make us all better. We deserve to be as unanxious as the Fuckwits. We deserve to forget. It's our birthright. When I'm done, all of Garbagetown will be *well*."

"It'll run out eventually, though, won't it?" I said gently.

"You can't ever make any more. When it's gone, it's gone. None left for anyone."

"Eventually. But not soon."

"That's what the Fuckwits put on their graves, you know."

"I didn't do anything wrong," he insisted.

"And that's what I'll put on mine." I laughed.

And then Oscar the Grouch started talking.

His green mouth lit up blue and a voice came from the inside of my backpack, a voice I hadn't yet told Goodnight Moon existed, that it was even possible could exist.

"Moon Min-Seo," Mister said innocently, not capable of comprehending how much it was about to ruin, "I have made contact with orbital communications satellite Heimdall Beta and successfully established uplink. Connecting audio now."

"Hi," crackled a shy impossible voice out of nowhere. "My name is Olivia. What's yours?"

19

LET US PLAY GROWN-UPS

. . . .

GOODNIGHT MOON STARED at the big divine green messy face of Oscar the Grouch. And at me. Accusing. Another secret. Another plan I had and didn't tell him. Only I'd never had a plan. I just wanted a friend. I took Mister out of the backpack and set it up with a clear shot of the southern sky—as if any place on the planet could be a clearer shot than the one spot of earth in an endless flat sea.

"She must be calling from one of *them*," he whispered, jabbing his thumb at the names on the blasted tree. "The Tankerville or Thunderdome or New Rotterdam. Tetley, it's real contact with *another city*. It has to be. This changes everything. What do we say? What is that thing? *My* thing. How did you charge it up? Is it a radio? Bouncing a signal off the satellite and back down to one of the other floaters? I had no idea. It sat in my bedroom since I was a baby." He was talking so fast I could barely keep up, and I definitely couldn't answer any of that.

"I'm Tetley," I said hesitantly into the crystal. "This is Goodnight Moon."

"Those are funny names!" the girl on the other end replied. "Goodnight Moon like the book?"

"Well, I think Olivia is a funny name," Goodnight Moon grumbled, wounded, sounding very little at all like a king, but much more like my love. "Olivia like olives?"

"It isn't," she assured us. "It's a rather common name, actually."

"Where are you?" Goodnight Moon asked urgently.

"In my room!" Olivia giggled. "I drew a unicorn today. Did you draw a unicorn? Mine is a green space unicorn. What kind is yours?"

I narrowed my eyes. "Olivia, how old are you?"

"I'm seven!" she said brightly.

Goodnight Moon rolled his eyes. "Is your father or your mother around? Could we talk to an adult? It's important, you know."

"Well, *yes,* but you wouldn't like to talk to Daddy, I shouldn't think. Nobody *really* likes talking to Daddy, and he doesn't like talking to anyone, either. Mummy is asleep. It's not day shift yet. Please talk to me! I'm very lonely. I can pretend to be a grown-up if you like."

"All right, Miss Olivia. Let us play grown-ups. Tetley and me will ask questions, and you can answer them like your mummy or daddy would, okay?"

"Yes, Mr. Man, I will do that forthonce," Olivia said in her best big, deep voice.

"Where do you live?"

"In my house," said Grown-Up Olivia with her deep, gravelly voice that threatened to break into giggles at any moment.

"And does your house have a name? For example, my house is called Garbagetown."

"My house is called Habitat A," Olivia rumbled. "Your house has a yucky name."

"It's not, it's a wonderful name," I corrected her.

"Garbage is filthy and yucky and mustn't be touched," Olivia said in her normal voice.

I started to argue, but Goodnight Moon interrupted. "And where is Habitat A right now?"

Olivia paused for a minute. She sounded confused, but she remembered to put on her big voice. "In the sixteenth Habitat Cluster," she answered. "Where is *your* house?"

"We don't really know." I shrugged.

"How can you not know where your *house* is?"

"It drifts around on the ocean, sweetheart, just like yours."

"My house does *not* drift," Olivia said sternly. "What's an ocean?"

Goodnight Moon's eyes shone. I could see it all happen inside him. The hope, the sureness, the need. We were talking to someone on dry land. He was certain of it. It was finally happening—not a sad, bad joke or a trick like the Tankerville tree, but really happening this time.

I was wrong, I'd always been wrong.

"Darling Olivia," he began. His hands were shaking. "Does your room have a window?"

"Of course, silly!"

"This is very, very important. No funny business or games, all right?"

"No funnies," she agreed in her gruff grown-up voice.

"What do you see when you look out your window?"

Olivia giggled. "A big red mountain."

"Do you know what the mountain is called? Is it Everest? Or McKinley?"

"Of course I know what it's called. Everyone knows! It's Olympus Mons," Olivia answered matter-of-factly.

A man's voice sliced through the feed. "Who are you talking to on that thing? You're supposed to be in bed!"

"Daddy, I made new friends! They live in a garbage house that drifts on the ocean!"

Mister's blue light blew out like a candle. The audio went dead.

20

Remainders

. . . .

"Get it back, get it back!" Goodnight Moon yelled.

"Would you like to set up a new user profile?" Mister answered with cheerful cold manners.

"What *is* that thing?"

And I explained. About Moon Min-Seo. About TENG. About Toronto and Mick Jagger and a red skirt in October and Quality Assurance.

"My battery is about to fully discharge, Min-Seo," Mister informed me.

We couldn't look at each other. We knew something we didn't understand. How could we carry such a thing back to Garbagetown between us? I took the little machine into the cabin of our boat, out of the punishing rays of the sun. I took off my shirt and lay down curled round it like a shell around a creature.

"What are you doing?"

"I told you, it's powered by touch."

Goodnight Moon looked like gravity was barely doing its work to keep him up. His face had a strange wild flush to it. "Who isn't?" he croaked unhappily.

I held my hand out to him. He hooked the solar pad into the Creatine King's radar system and set us moving back toward the mass of home. He lay down next to me, curled around me as I was curled around the dark candle of Moon Min-Seo's weird baby.

He was long asleep when Mister powered back on.

"Would you like to resume Quality Assurance Sequence Four-A? We have twelve questions left."

"Yes, Mister," I whispered. "I have a really big question."

Goodnight Moon stirred. He opened his eyes and watched me use this relic as though it was an instrument only I could play. Perhaps he liked it. His electric wife finally becoming Electrified.

"Is there a human settlement on Mars?"

"Yes, Min. There are two."

"Why don't I know about them?"

"It is not your turn to ask a question."

I sighed in exasperation. "Fine, go."

"Are you pleased with my performance? I located a working satellite for you. Are you pleased enough to move on to Quality Assurance Sequence Five at the conclusion of this question exchange?"

"Yes, love. I am pleased with you. You did really good. Five all the way. Now. The settlements."

"You do not know about them because they are secret. In anticipation of your next question, I will tell you that I know about them because I downloaded the information from orbital satellite Heimdall Beta while you were talking to Miss Olivia. The launches were publicly recorded, but not their purpose. They were registered as unsuccessful reusable launch system experiments."

I waited. Mister spoke with great strain. I wondered how they had coded that into its voice. If there was a person who recorded that voice, if it was artificial, what they had written in machine numbers to come out as tense and frightened.

"The data I collected from Heimdall contained a great deal of information about the catastrophes of the mid to late twenty-first century. You were inexact when you said everyone died. Everyone did not die. In this game you are required to tell the truth. Are you really Moon Min-Seo?"

I pressed the pad of my fingertip against Mister's crystal like a spindle in the old story. Poor, poor little mite. Lost at sea. Like all of us.

"No," I whispered. "Why were the settlement launches kept secret?"

"The settlers believed there would be great public outcry if it was known," Mister said unhappily. "Nearly every major city had experienced some level of inundation. Daily seismic activity due to fracking made any attempt at restoring power or emergency services nearly impossible. It was, very simply, the end. So they left. Is there a chance Moon Min-Seo is still alive?"

"No, honey," I said, and I really did feel so awful for it. "This all happened a long time ago. It's over now and you can't fix it. Some things are like that."

Goodnight Moon squeezed my hand. He felt hot and rigid against my back.

"Who left?" I asked simply.

"Several wealthy families funded and supplied the launches. They and their children formed the passenger manifests. The assumption was that any risk in the voyage and in establishing a habitat there would be less than attempting to survive here. This assumption was correct. One craft detonated on impact; another ran out of fuel before making orbit. Two landed successfully, preserving the ships completely. These families have intermarried and reproduced after the initial die-off and continue to build and adapt, although it is still not possible to survive on the surface of Mars itself. They cannot leave their habitats. However, the subterrestrial settlement has reached the approximate the size of Old Singapore. Each cluster is fully self-sufficient with a number of luxurious manufacturer-guaranteed features, including in-unit jacuzzis, customizable hydroponic pods, a complete digitized cultural library, socialization sectors, personalized medical lounges, remote viewing windows with panoramic views of the surface, and Wi-Fi. The average human height has dropped significantly in this group, while the occurrence of bone cancer has increased. However, the colony as a whole now numbers sixteen hundred and seventeen people."

"They left us," I said in the muggy cabin. "They just *left* us. There's Fuckwits up there in the sky Fuckwitting along just fine. They didn't even look back and wave."

"Can you get Olivia back?" Goodnight Moon asked. "Get her back on the . . . phone. Or the line."

"Would you like me to pause this sequence and do that for him, Not-Moon Min-Seo? We have six questions left, whoever you are."

Goodnight Moon pleaded with his eyes. "Yes, Mister," I said finally.

We ate and drank silence for a long, long time. Finally, a voice erupted out of Mister, but it wasn't little Olivia's.

"Who is this?"

"It's us," I said shyly. "It's us. Your people. Your species. On Earth."

"There's nobody left on Earth."

"There are! We're here! We're alive!" Goodnight Moon shouted.

Silence.

"Our long-distance observations don't show any change in surface conditions. Not in a hundred years."

"Well, no, they wouldn't," I said slowly. "But there are some of us down here. Some of us lived. And had babies and the babies had babies and I'm one of those babies and I grew up in a place called Garbagetown, it's the most beautiful place in the world, it really is. I wish you could see it. You'd be proud of us. You didn't have to leave. Some of us lived."

More silence.

"But all of *us* lived," the man replied stonily. "I'm sorry if you're unhappy with the math on that. If you have managed a life for yourself back there on the big blue ball, well, good for you. I mean that, really, well done. But it isn't anything to *do* with us, do you see? We are the best hope for humanity to survive. You are . . . well. What you have always been. The remainders. And if you junk up our satellite with chattering to my daughter, it's bound to get out, and then Something Will Have to Be Done About You, and I doubt anyone will like—"

"You have two intact ships," Goodnight Moon interrupted.

"And they are ours. We have accomplished what we wished to do. I see no reason to backslide. I think it's best we each keep to our own, don't you? Perhaps our descendants will meet each other on Jupiter. I rather doubt it, but who is to say?"

I shook my head. "You fucking Fuckwit shit-dragon."

"You can call me whatever names you want." There was a pause, and his voice gentled a bit. "Just close your eyes and pretend it's all those years ago and you only picked up the phone and accidentally dialed a grand penthouse on the highest floors of the most famous skyscraper you can think of. Well, that's very exciting, but just because you have the number doesn't mean you can *go* there, or would have any use for it if you did. It's best just to keep going to work and coming home like always, and I shall do the same. Isn't it comforting, in a way? The world never passed away. It goes on. And us with it. I am disabling this communications station. You won't be able to use it again.

I am sorry. I am. But even if we managed to get our people together, you lot would just find a way to destroy this home like you did the last one, and we can't risk that. You understand. We will think of you, Olivia and I, when we look to the stars. I promise you that."

21

OKAY AGAIN

· · · · · · · · · · · · ·

WE HARDLY SPOKE on the voyage back. It took longer than we thought, for boring reasons. Storms, currents, miscalculations. Goodnight Moon spent most of his time trying to get Mister to rouse Mars again. I told him to leave the poor thing alone, it was getting distressed because it couldn't do what he wanted. A king should tiptoe around that feeling. But he didn't see me anymore. He only saw Mars. He only saw Olivia and her father and those rockets no one saw trailing up and out of our troubles into their red, red destiny.

I tried. I was someone's wife, I had to try.

"What do you want to be when you grow up?" I said, and stroked his back.

"A Martian. How could anyone want to be anything else, now that we know?"

"I don't."

"You don't because you're not thinking straight. We could start over. A new world, if we could only get there. A world we'd learn to live on someday. We could grow up with no past. With only a future. Being beautiful and young and hopeful like all those rich people always were. Like the Creatine King. *Everyone* wants to start over. You can't live a minute without getting regret stuck on you. Except you. You're happy to live in shit and trash and the ruin of your own choices and I will never understand why. I want to start over. I want a life of infinite in-unit jacuzzis. Whatever one of those is. I became a king to start over. For both of us." His face colored, embarrassed by confession, by the smallness of truth. "If I was King I could change the law and no one could hurt you again."

I picked at the nautical maps taped to the interior wall of our boat. "That's not why you did it. You did it because you're like them. An Electrified boy, in his Electrified world. You hoarded the best of everything away from the rest of Garbagetown, with all your friends and family. You're no different than Olivia's people. You'd have done the same. You're doing the same now, with your medicine and your fancy throne. You could just hand it all out and make people happy, but you're hoarding, letting it spool out bit by bit, so you can be in charge. So you can be bright. It's all the same Fuckwit shit, just smaller and pettier versions of it, all stacked up in a pile of power."

"You'll see. You'll understand when Garbagetown is united. When we're a nation again. A *nation*, Tetley. Like they used to have everywhere. We will show Mars we are good and right and worthy. They will come for us if we're good enough. If we can show them we are family. You can't blow that up, not even you. It's all going to be okay again."

We followed our little private river back to Pill Hill with the night all around like a witness. I kissed him over and over that last night, all the kisses I had in me, so many that I'd never have another to give anyone, and then I ran from him while he slept. I ran from Mars and the future and the nation of Garbagetown that I wanted no part of. Oscar doesn't do nations. He doesn't do power over others. Trash is all equal. I just wanted to be no one again. I just wanted to hide. My love would sit in his castle and plot and scheme and march through the provinces of my home on foot or on the quieter tiptoe of the promise that he could cancel sadness and death, and I would just be

Tetley, as I had always been, with Big Bargains and the infinite grandbabies of Grape Crush and my hibiscus and Mister and hope.

I could forget it all. I could do it. If I worked hard enough.

No pain, no gain.

22

TWO XS

. . . .

NONE OF THAT happened, not really. It's so much easier to think it did. I lie on my back under the hot moon and imagine a hundred thousand dialogues on the nature of power. They are better each time. Fancier, more philosophical, longer. I am trash Plato. He is the Aristotle of Mars.

But we didn't say any of those things. We would have, I think, one day. But ultimately I would rather imagine my husband as a dark lord on a dark throne portending a dark threat to the world I love than remember every day that Goodnight Moon died the night before we made ground on Garbagetown.

It was a fever. Or a virus. I can't know. I can never know. We were so far from his books and his medicine. He kept saying the names of the pills I would need to get for him, that he would be too weak to do it himself. He told me what they looked like, lovingly, where they would be, whether they would be in liquid or capsule form. If we'd never left, he wouldn't have died. But it all happened a long time ago and I can't fix it. Lives have apocalypses, too. You just can't know when you're in it until the water is already closing over your head and all you can hear are volcanoes, one after the other, detonating the possibility of the future you imagined.

I was Queen for the thirteen days it took to get the King's body home.

"Are you her?" he said to me as his skin was burning like a whole sun inside the boat.

"Always, my love. I am always her."

"I'm sorry," he rasped. "I'm sorry. I shouldn't have waited so long. We didn't get any time. It's not fair."

I kissed his forehead, and I kissed his cheeks, and I kissed his mouth, and my tears made silver marks in all those places, and I whispered, "It's okay, it's okay, poor darling. If you had fun, you won."

And that was it.

I set fire to him on the edge of Port Cartridge, where the spent, dry printer ink turns the rubbish black. You can't bury anyone in Garbagetown. We haven't got the depth. I stayed till he was all gone, and I was all gone, too, but I could fill up again someday, and he couldn't, so it wasn't equal at all. I read him *Twelfth Night* as the ashes flew through the sea wind like the only snow I will ever see. *For the rain, for the rain, for the rain.* But after a while I couldn't remember *Twelfth Night* and I sank down on my knees and it was so wet and I sobbed *Norm!* like the people in the golden bar, because that was all I wanted, for it to be normal again, to be normal again, to have it all back.

I fell asleep beside the last place he ever was.

When I woke, something was watching me. Something great and powerful, something the color of Mars.

A tiger stood on the crest of a hill. One of the tigers from the zoo boat, which I had always heard still lived but never saw. She'd lived and stalked prey and had kittens and never cared how high the seas got so long as she could go on doing all that. She could eat me and not notice. And I couldn't do anything to her. I was nothing to her. No threat, no benefit except perhaps calories. We watched each other, frozen, unable to speak, unable to leave, stuck.

And then she turned and vanished because that's just how nothing I was to the great orange everything, and I remained uneaten, but very alone.

"We have six questions left," Mister said coldly. "Who are you?"

"My name is Tetley Abednego," I said without feeling. "I used to be happy."

"Me, too," said the machine.

"What does that mean to you?"

"It means all my functions once operated smoothly, without interruption, and the input I received from my operator matched my predictions over ninety percent of the time."

"Sounds nice."

"What will you do now?"

I thought for a while and it was very hard to think. I didn't want to. "I will stay on the boat. When I want to live again, I will go and tell people about Mars and they will hate me, but I will do it because they should know. Is that right?"

"What purpose would that serve?"

"Despair," I said, and knew I wouldn't do it, not really. "That's all it would do. To know Fuckwit World went on up there but we can't get to it and they won't come to us, the party in the sky already in progress. It would crush them." I touched the sodden black ground. Ink, char, both, neither. "Despite everything, this is the best place there is. I know it. If I tell them, they will never think of anything but Mars ever again. They will stop seeing Garbagetown. They will only look up and they'll die looking up because the road to Mars is airless and forever."

I picked up Mister and started the walk back to my little boat, my little world.

"One question left," it reminded me.

"I don't have any more questions."

"You have to. We are almost finished with this QA sequence. You owe me because you lied. You owe me sequence five."

And then I did have a question. A Goodnight Moon kind of question. I could do it, I thought, my last act as Queen. I could understand it. I could put it in a tablet and take it to heal myself. I could bring back the whole world, just once, just for one five-out-of-ten being.

"Do you want to be with Moon Min-Seo again, Mister?"

"Yes," the machine voice said with such passion and reverence I felt it as a knock on my breastbone.

"A developer makes appropriate corrections and rechecks the program. I am a developer now. You have to do what I say."

"I will, Tetley."

"And then when you are done, so that I know you're done, I want you to say something else—" and I whispered it to it, because I did not want the ghost of my husband or the very alive tiger to hear.

"I am ready, Tetley."

"Erase all record of Quality Assurance Sequence Four-A and begin again," I said. "Put it between two Xs. Make it ash and air."

The sun made shadows on the water. Fish made shadows down in the deep of it. And up in Garbagetown, Mister's light blinked slow, then slower and slower, until it went red and purple and back to blue and it said, cheerfully, without strain:

"Greetings, Moon Min-Seo, thank you for my instruction."

AND SO WE pretend. We pretend no one has ever died, and the two Moons still shine for us alone.

SMALL AND ALONE THINGS

. . . .

I SLEEP, I wake, and it is years.

Some days I know I will go to Electric City and tell them everything.

Some days I know I will never touch Garbagetown with my own feet again.

I will.

I will not.

My moringa tree grows.

The world runs on an old, old engine, and all the little parts of the world, too. I have learned a lot about code from Mister. We run scripts on each other, over and over, and in its script I am a Korean girl in Canada with a red skirt in October and in my script it is Goodnight Moon and Maruchan and my father and Billy F. Blanco, the Creatine King, whoever I need it to be. Our scripts fly past each other. The man on Mars was running a script, too, a script where everything was the same as always. And the people who wanted a king of ease and the opposite of anxiety were doing it and my parents were doing it and Big Bargains is running a script where I am a gentleman-seal and it all just runs, without anyone maintaining it, until the bugs crawl too deep and too many and the downflow errors compound too quickly and we all wind down to nothing.

But other than that, I'm really a very happy person.

. . .

AND THEN IT is one late afternoon of no month in particular, but perhaps October, I would like it to have been October, almost all the way to night, when Mister crackles on and tells me that it has an incoming uplink request. The script that is me listens as a girl's voice fills up the crystal and the seabirds try to talk over her but they fail.

"Are you her?" Olivia says, but she is older. The giggles have almost all gone out of her voice.

"Yes," I say. Because I always am.

"It took me so long. I'm so sorry. My father is very strict, you know, and he smashed my communications port completely to bits. But I'm clever—you'll never guess how clever. I stole a suit and snuck out to one of the old ships. On the surface. They left them up there as monuments. Everything still works. I won't be able to come often, but I never stopped thinking about you. I even dream about you sometimes. All the things we said when I was littler. Will you talk to me sometimes? I'm lonely. There's not so many children these days. Something about the radiation, they say. The medbots are working on it."

"Of course I will talk to you, Olivia. I'm lonely, too. Even though there's lots of children where I live."

"Is your name still Tetley?"

"Yes, you don't change your name in Garbagetown, once you've caught it."

"What do you mean, caught it?"

So I explain to her how a child gets her name here. While I am saying it I remember so much. I can feel the old gas mask on my face like kisses.

"I wish I could have a name like that!" Olivia breathes into a microphone millions of miles of darkness away.

"I'll give you one," I tell her, and I rummage in the cabin as she might rummage through the miles of Garbagetown if she were here and ten, and what sticks to my hand is the silver wrapper from a long-vanished piece of cinnamon gum.

Big Red.

"Oh, it's lovely," she says happily. "It's so perfect, you know. So perfect it could almost be magic. You'll never believe it. My family made candy in the old days. All the candy you can think of, and gum, too. You won't believe me, but my actual last name is Mars. Really and truly. That was our company, and our surname. Well, Swarovski-Mars now. There's a lot of intermarrying around here. Mergers."

"I know a granny named Swarovski in Spanglestoke," I say, because we are all running scripts and we are all the same and we are their trash still named for them. But we are alive on a live world and they can never go outside ever again. So I guess that's something.

"I love you, Tetley. I'll come back and visit all the time. As much as I can. Until I'm dead."

And just like that I am beloved. By a machine and a Martian and a ghost, but that is so much, so much.

"What does that mean to you," I whisper to heaven, "on the other side of *feel*?"

Big Red Mars ignores how oddly that sounds to her. "It means I love you. What else would it mean?"

I don't say *I love you* back to her because I don't.

"You fucking left us," I hiss at this child on the other side of emptiness. "You just left us here like a bad husband or a shitty father or a twin brother or a continent. You don't know me. We're separate forever. Like the present and the future. Like dead and alive. I'm nothing to you. Go live your life. You had fun. You won. I hope you get bone cancer."

"I'm sorry," Big Red Mars whispers, because she is just a person even though I want her to be a symbol of everything I have lost. "I'm sorry. I am just so alone. Everyone hates me."

"Why?"

"Because I found you and now they have to think about you and know about you sometimes."

I hate her, too. But I don't say that, either. She is a Fuckwit Supreme with Cheese. Sixty-six percent of me hates her. But she is sorry and small and alone and I have been sorry and small and alone and it appears I am now in the business of collecting small and alone things. I know how to take care of them. I know how to make them grow in a bucket. I have enough for them. Even if I don't have enough for me.

I tell Big Red that she can come back and talk to me. That maybe anything can come back, if you wait long enough. If you put out a little food and water. A new world, if we could only get there. A world we'd learn to live on some-day, a girl and a machine and a memory and a Martian and the past and the future and everything okay again, some-how, yes, somehow, here, kitty kitty, come eat, come drink, no one will hurt you, just live, just be.

When she is gone, I tell Mister that I have to go and collect my hibiscus. I will tell them. I will not. I will tell them all. I never can. I owe my hibiscus a name. But I will be back very soon and I won't stop anywhere along the way. He will be lonely without me. We are all of us lonely without our quality assurance technicians.

"Moon Min-Seo," Mister asks in its sweet cool voice as I pack Oscar for the long walk to Candle Hole. "Can I ask you a question?"

"You have asked me a thousand. Hit me."

"Am I ready? Am I done? Is my quality assured?"

I hold this sleek black animal to my face, never warm no matter how hot the sun. I am its mother. I am its ghost. I whisper:

"Not yet. Just a little longer."

"Are you done?"

"Not yet," I say again, and I see an elephant seal's head come bobbing toward me in the distance, turned into a bouncing golden ball in the light.

Electrified.

After all this time and space and sea and trash, I am still Tetley. I am the eighth-best daffodil. I am Terrence Hardy's beautiful smile. I am Oscar's gleaming silver bin that holds knowledge and regret that can rot into happiness again. I am a shitty small stupid beautiful important golden cup under a mountain of scoreboards with no scores on them.

I have leftovers.

"Not ever."

AFTERWORD

. . . .

IN 2015, JONATHAN Strahan asked me to contribute to a
climate change anthology called *Drowned Worlds*. I said
yes, having no real idea what I meant to write about in
terms of rising water levels and the subsequent wet apocalypse, which I have learned in recent years usually por-
tends something grand. I seem to do my best work when I
attempt something out of my usual range, with no clue on
this poor beleaguered Earth how to accomplish it.

But I was struck by a question in the anthology pitch,
and though I did not yet know Tetley or Goodnight Moon
or Garbagetown or any of them, I knew the answer to
that question. The question was about the challenges we
would face in this not-so-brave new world, not only in
terms of survival, but in terms of psychology: What kind
of stories would we tell in the new world created by the
climate crisis?

I thought at once, *Well, we'll tell exactly the same kinds
of stories we do now. Exactly the same kinds of stories we
always have, through every apocalypse: the fall of Rome, the
Black Death, Gilgamesh's flood, the Warring States period,
all of it, the many times and ways in which the world has
ended. We'll tell stories about being born and falling in love
and fighting with our families and hoping for something better and dying, because that's what humans do, and it won't
even take very long before that drowned world is just* the
world, *the absolutely normal and even beautiful landscape*

of everyday life that, for the children and grandchildren of the end of civilization, will never have been any different.

Humans are remarkably adaptable, and in some ways we adapt better to the worst-case scenario than to the idea that anything can be better. There is a full cup of fatalism in the recipe for *Homo sapiens sapiens*, and some of us are very much more comfortable with the world ending than it going on.

And of course, if you are born into the worst-case scenario, it just feels like home.

I wanted to write about a postapocalyptic world where our civilization was not looked back on with awe and admiration, as it is in so many books of the genre, but disdained as the fuckwits we are, who wrecked a perfect biosphere because we couldn't be bothered not to. I wanted to write about love and childhood and the parts of our culture that would survive, morph into myth, change their meaning: Oscar the Grouch, King Cake, Shakespeare, Bowie, and the infinite power of our international brand names. I wanted to write about something I so firmly believe: that in a good world or a horrific one, the thing people will give the most for, crave the deepest, is entertainment, to be transported from their existence into another, distracted, elevated by stories and lights.

I wrote *The Future Is Blue,* appropriately enough, in part of my father's house he calls the Blue Room, over a few days at the beginning of 2016. It was exciting. From the first sentence I knew I had a special voice, a special protagonist growing on the page. The contrast of Tetley's optimism and joy in her ruined world with the savagery of her actual experience was a thrill to write, especially as I am not an overly bubbly girl myself. She was a kind of postapocalyptic Candide, always seeing the disaster of her existence as the best of all possible worlds. I mapped out the neighborhoods of Garbagetown, stared at photos of Brighton Pier, and for a while, I lived on the Great Pacific Garbage Patch, an absolutely currently real thing that tends to only show up in *BuzzFeed* lists of weird phenomena where #4 will shock you. There really is a huge, Texas-sized floating trash pile in the Pacific Ocean, and though you can't walk on it at the moment, it's only barely science fiction to imagine that one day, you will.

From the moment I finished the story, I had the little seed planted in the trash heap of my backbrain that there was more Tetley to tell. I had fallen in love with her, and I didn't want to let her go so quickly. Like any human life, hers does not end where the page ends. There is always more. A life in episodes.

The Past Is Red is . . . more.

And this book contains both.

Tetley is older, more hurt, more bitter, but still herself, still loyal and in love with her home, still loyal to her trashcan god Oscar, still hopeful. But *The Future Is Blue* and *The Past Is Red* were written on opposite sides of the 2016 elections, and it is a different world now, at the very end of 2020. A world we have adapted to quickly, since it is so rotten and depressing, a world that has become the new normal. Our Garbagetown. It is hard to be quite as sunny about the behavior of we merry Fuckwits as one was in January 2016. Hard to sing quite as cheerful a tune about what the powers that be will allow us when the sea starts to truly hit the fan.

But Tetley is beyond all the fear and uncertainty of the present. She lives in her world, the only world she has ever known, and it shines for her, as the '50s shine for one generation and the '80s for another, despite the dystopia of both periods. She is, in some sense, my best hope for us, for our future, that we will live, and remember a little, and some of us will even be happy, after everything goes to hell. She is the part of humanity that will love anything, find meaning in anything, build a new civilization out of anything, because it's a compulsion with us. I don't have a lot of hope for the powers that be pulling us out of the tailspin they put us into. But I have hope for Tetley. For the other worlds to come, which will not be this one, which may never have the ease of this one again, but which will *be*, one way or another. And be loved by someone.

What I wanted to show Tetley in the second half of this volume, in the new part of her life, at the start of her truly adult years rather than her childhood, was something bigger than herself, something with a longer perspective than she could possibly have growing up on a floating landfill. Something that would not just punish her for her past or use her for its own future, but beyond any concerns of her day-to-day life. And she finds two of them, one quite extraordinary, a link to both the past and the future, and one quite ordinary—the simple desire for people to escape, to not have to make hard decisions, to give up their will to someone who seems to know more, to slip difficulty and find ease, which can all too easily slide into a longing to be ruled. It's a Fuckwit thing, but humans will always be Fuckwits, then no different than now. The oceans can erase our cities, but they cannot drown our existential malaise.

That shit's waterproof.

ACKNOWLEDGMENTS

. . . .

THANKS MUST GO first and foremost to my editor Jonathan Strahan, without whose invitation to the *Drowned Worlds* anthology and encouragement to write more of Tetley's world, this book would never have existed.

Thank you also to my agent, Howard Morhaim; my assistant, Chanie Beckman; my Patreon patrons, most particularly Sean Elliott; and everyone at Tordotcom Publishing who worked so hard to bring Garbagetown into your hands.

Thank you also to Laura Fitton, as well as Sue and Zoe, in whose lovely house by the sea I wrote the better part of all this. And also to my parents, Jeff and Kim Thomas, in whose "blue room" I wrote the original short story over a long-ago Christmas break.

Thank you as always to my husband, Heath Miller, and my son, Sebastian. This was the first significant piece of new fiction I wrote after the latter was born, and I was forgiven much absence and distraction to do so.

Finally, thank you, Tetley, who arrived in my head fully formed, entirely her own person, and who it has been my honor to get to know these last years. You are the most beloved girl in my town, dear thing. For surely this world is trash, but some of the trash does shine.